FULL MOONS, DUNES & MACAROONS

A COZY WITCH MYSTERY

ERIN JOHNSON

For all the ladies. You deserve the best.

And in loving memory of
Grandpa Webb— happy birthday.
I will carry on your memory by striving to be
as cheerful as you always were.

YOU'RE READING BOOK 5? YOU MUST BE INTO THIS SERIES!

Make sure you don't miss anything!
Sign up for the Erin Johnson Writes newsletter
at
www.ErinJohnsonWrites.com

As a thank you for signing up, you'll receive
Imogen's Spellbook
a free book of illustrated recipes featured in
The Spells & Caramels Series.

LIQUID FEAST

I shifted on the crocheted fuchsia pouf that I sat on and squirmed to get comfortable. I leaned closer to Maple beside me and lowered my voice. "My left cheek is numb."

She chuckled and pulled her skirt lower over her thighs. She sat with her legs tucked to the side of her own pouf. "I should not have worn a dress tonight." She sighed sadly. "No one told me not to wear a dress."

I shot her a sympathetic look. Luckily, I'd opted to wear white cropped pants with a floral-embroidered white camisole. I could at least sit cross-legged.

The man standing before us droned on, a champagne flute embellished with rubies in one hand. "I still remember when cousin Shaday took out that guard by whacking him behind the knee with her wooden sword... and she was only four! Watch out, Hank, she's always been a feisty one."

A twitter of laughter rose from the guests who sat at the long, low tables that formed three sides of a square, with the royal table on a raised platform forming the fourth side. The cousin twirled his long mustache around a finger, pleased his joke had landed. *Kill me now*. My eyes darted to Hank. He sat in the center of the head table beside Shaday, their families flanking them. Both looked lovely and royal, the perfect couple.

Maple found my hand under the table and squeezed it. "You okay?"

Had my train of thought shown on my face? Something twisted in my chest, but I wrenched it down and took a deep breath. I forced a smile. "I'm at my boyfriend's engagement dinner to another woman, why wouldn't I be okay?" I gave a dry chuckle and Maple's frown deepened.

"No, really. I know you're tired of me asking, but—"

I sniffed and lifted my chin. "I'm fine, Maple."

She tilted her head and lifted a blonde brow, unconvinced.

I tried again. "Really. We're all adults. This wedding is just a formality and I've known it was coming since day one." I waved a hand, brushing it all off. Maybe if I told myself that enough times, I'd really believe it.

She pressed her mouth into a tight line and leaned closer. "Just because you know it's coming, doesn't mean you're prepared. I can't imagine how hard this must be."

Heat flushed across my chest, but I sat straighter and vowed to ignore it. "It's not that hard. Hank and I are fine, and I actually like Shaday. I just have to get through the ceremony, and then life will go back to normal." I sighed. "Well, a new normal."

Maple's eyes grew wider. "But where are they going to live? I mean, Shaday's been back here in the Fire Kingdom the last few months, but once they're together all the time, won't that make it harder for you and Hank?"

I swallowed, my throat tight. I really didn't want to talk about this, not now... not ever. Hank had been trying to broach the subject with me for weeks, but I always changed topics or ended our conversations abruptly. It was too painful. What I'd gathered though, was that Shaday, as the firstborn, would have become queen had she chosen to marry someone the Fire Kingdom tribes approved of, one of their own. By marrying Hank, she passed the right to rule to one of her younger brothers. When they grew older, of course. Currently they were in their early twenties and late teens.

So Hank wouldn't have to move to the Fire Kingdom permanently, but he'd have to visit for extended periods. He'd wanted to know if I'd come with him when that happened. I hadn't given him an answer yet. How would that work with my job at the bakery? How would I feel, being in a foreign land without my friends, as the girlfriend of a married man?

I shook my head—big questions, the kind that gave me headaches. And no one, including Hank, believed me when I said I didn't want to talk about them. I took a deep breath and let my shoulders drop.

I gave Maple's hand a squeeze back. "We can talk later, okay? Let's just have fun tonight." I willed my face to relax. "I really am okay."

Her blue eyes stayed worried, but her mouth quirked to the side. "All right. We can talk later."

I grinned and relaxed. "Good."

Shaday's cousin, giving what felt like the fiftieth toast of the night, paced before us in the open square between the tables. There had been a near constant parade of guests trying to outdo each other by presenting lavish gifts to the royal couple, followed by even more elaborate toasts to their health and happiness.

"Shaday has always been so kind, angelic even, to her

distant relations and I know that she will continue to be in her future with Hank...."

I rolled my eyes and leaned over. "This guy must want one huge favor."

Maple chuckled. "Or he's making up for a terrible present."

I smirked. "Yeah, he probably regifted them a toaster."

"A what?"

I giggled at Maple's drawn brows. "Human thing. I forgot." My stomach growled and I pressed my hands to my aching middle. "And whose idea was toasts *before* dinner? They ought to be punished."

Maple lifted her brows again at my tone and Iggy chuckled. My little magical flame munched on a stick of his favorite wood, linden. He burned inside a gold, Moroccan-style lamp that sat on the table nestled amongst the gold-rimmed glassware and little pots of jellies and spices.

"Yeah, you're totally fine." He cackled again and addressed Maple. "Just listen to her, she's starting to sound like me."

Maple shot me a look and paled. "Not good," she muttered to herself.

I rolled my eyes and leaned an elbow on the table, Iggy's golden heat warming my face. I'd been surprised to find the desert actually got chilly once the sun went down.

"No. If I were you, I'd be acting like normal me, because you're getting to eat. While hungry me is acting like normal you, because I'm starving and cranky." I sat back and folded my arms with a huff. "So unfair."

Iggy glared at me. "Unfair? You'd like to see me burn out, then? If I don't eat I extinguish, but apparently that's preferable to you becoming hangry, goddess forbid."

I shook my head at him. "You're so dramatic." I let out a

heavy sigh. "I mean, I like a liquid dinner as much as the next girl now and then, but I could use something solid with all this wine." I twirled the stem of my gold-rimmed wine-glass between my fingers.

Maple elbowed me and I looked up, startled, to find Shaday's third cousin twice removed, or whoever he was, staring at me. In fact, all four long tables, I mean, at least a hundred people at each one, staring at me. I gulped and ducked my head. "Sorry."

He lifted his hooked nose and continued. I stared at my lap, the back of my neck burning, until I felt everyone's collective attention shift away from me.

"Sorry," I whispered to Maple. "I didn't realize I was speaking so loudly. Maybe I am a little grumpier than I realized."

"Jud a lil?" Iggy said, his mouth full.

Blissfully, the cousin wrapped up his toast and lifted his glass. Murmurs and the swishing sound of shifting silk and taffeta filled the air as the hundreds of guests, and I, lifted our champagne flutes.

"To my dear cousin Shaday and her handsome beau, Prince Harry."

I lifted my chin and downed the glass in one gulp. The bubbly liquid left my mouth dry and my head light. Maple gripped the edge of the table, and the gold and red silk tablecloth bunched between her fingers.

"I think one more toast and I'll be beyond tipsy." She swayed slightly and Wiley, sitting on her other side, slid an arm around her shoulders to steady her.

"Whoa, there. You just need some food."

Maple patted his hand, which rested on her shoulder.

"We all do," I grumbled. Iggy gave a happy moan as he

munched his third split log of the night and I glared at him. Not fair.

As the cousin made his way down the head table, bowing and hugging and shaking hands with Shaday's younger brothers and then her parents, Amelia, dressed in her signature white, spoke to Hank. He looked so handsome in his royal finery, complete with a blue-and-gold sash. Even among all the glittering jewels, silky gowns, and glowing lanterns, Hank stood out.

He looked handsome and composed, and had kind words for everyone—though he must be as exhausted and starving as all of us. I grinned when I spotted Francis hovering behind him—literally. The vampire's toes dangled a couple of inches above a beautiful rug which lay atop soft desert sand. Tall, thin, and pale, he seemed to glow in the moonlight. He wore his long black hair slicked back from his face. He yawned, and with his mouth open wide, I glimpsed his needle-sharp, catlike fangs.

He blinked his jet-black eyes and looked as bored as I was. I cocked my head to the side. His cat eyeliner looked better than mine. I wondered if Rhonda had done it for him. With Francis roped into bodyguard duty by Hank's father, King Roch, to whom he was beholden, Rhonda sat with us, a few seats down on my right. I leaned back and glanced past Wiley to her. She swayed slightly, a half-empty wine glass in each hand. I grinned. She, at least, was enjoying her "dinner."

I looked back up at the head table and my shoulders slumped as my eyes slid to Shaday. Her long black locks tumbled in tight curls over her bare shoulders, her dark eyes glowing against her tan face and the spattering of freckles that made her so uniquely beautiful. She spoke then, and ducked her chin as the cousin threw his head back and laughed. Maybe they *were* close, and I was just being cynical.

I dropped my eyes to my lap and clenched my hands together. I shouldn't even be here tonight. Wool and the other Fire Kingdom bakers moved among the tables, refilling glasses of champagne, wine, and orange blossom lemonade, helping out the kitchen staff. Which was where we would have been, had Hank not insisted that I and the other bakers were his friends and deserved places at the table. My stomach clenched.

I didn't deserve this. I'd been nothing but negative and grumpy all night. And if I didn't even deserve a seat at the table, how could I deserve Hank?

"Hi, Imogen."

I jerked and looked up.

Wool's dark eyes, like pools of chocolate, stared down at me. "I didn't mean to startle you."

Even his voice reminded me of the treat, smooth and rich and velvety. No wonder Maple was into him. Well, that and his lush curly hair, handsome face, and broad shoulders. I forced a smile and hoped my dark thoughts from a moment ago hadn't been written all over my face.

"Hi, Wool. No, that's all right."

"She must have drifted into a starvation-induced coma." Iggy clicked his tongue and shook his head in mock sympathy.

Wool took a knee to address my flame and grinned. "Damavash flames are always the fieriest."

"Ha!" Iggy burst out in cackles. He turned to me, then Maple and Wiley and all the other bakers beside us. "Did you hear? Oh man! This guy. Did you hear, Annie? *Fiery!* So funny." He shot Wiley a pointed look. "Wool is the best."

A smile played at the edges of Wool's handsome mouth. "You remember me, little flame?"

Iggy grew deadly serious. "You saved me." He half-turned and shot me a look. "When that one almost let me extinguish." He glowed brighter. "I will always remember you for that, always."

Wool chuckled. "It was not such a thing, Ignatius."

"Ignatius?" I burst out, before I could stop myself.

The little fire rounded on me and puffed himself bigger and brighter. "That's my name. So what?"

My jaw dropped. "Ignatius is your name?" My mouth worked a couple of times before I could get another word out. "How did I not know this?" I gaped at Iggy. "And what does a Damavash flame mean?"

Wool cleared his throat, a deep sound. "My apologies. I did not realize Iggy was your preferred name." He looked at me. "I asked him his true name for the spell I used to revive him during the competition."

Iggy turned in his lantern. "Oh, psh. Ignatius is great, you can call me whatever you want."

Oh, wow. Someone was fangirling *hard*. I grinned. "Okay... Ignatius."

Iggy whipped around and narrowed his eyes. "I said *he* could call me that."

I fought a grin. "Are you embarrassed?"

Iggy huffed. "No, geez. It's just that when *Wool* says it, it sounds cool."

I bit my lip to keep from laughing outright, and nudged Maple under the table. Wool rose and refilled my glass of lemonade from a giant golden pitcher.

"And a Damavash flame," Iggy continued, "to answer your question, is the best kind of flame."

Wool's eyes sparkled but he nodded his agreement. "It's true. You have a special fire there, Imogen."

Iggy whispered, "He called me special," his eyes wide and round.

I rolled my eyes. "He certainly is."

"Damavash flames come from Damavash Volcano." Wool tilted his head to the side. I looked left across the sandy valley towards the looming shadow in the near distance. The tall mountain was only visible in the night because of the glowing blue veins that laced through it.

"Why does it glow blue?" Maple asked.

Wool filled her glass with orange blossom lemonade. Henna-like tattoos wound over the back of his right hand and up his wrist—the traditional tattoo of the Fire Kingdom. K'ree had told me that when people from the Fire Kingdom married, a special artist merged each person's tattoos to create a new pattern, that was tattooed on their other hand. My stomach sank. Would Hank be getting a tattoo to match Shaday's when they married in three days?

"There is a story our people like to tell," Wool continued. "Called the legend of Damavash."

Wiley folded his arms and scoffed. "Sounds like a kids' story."

Iggy rounded on him. "Insult him again and I'll burn you."

Wiley's eyes widened and his lip curled. "Sea snakes!"

"Yeah, Iggy," I muttered. "Take it down a notch."

Wool chuckled. "It isn't an insult. It *is* a children's story, but many believe it's based in truth. The legend goes that long ago, the mountain was just a mountain and Damavash a young man who lived in the city at its base. But when the monsters were driven from the wilds, a great serpent of fire named Tar claimed the mountain as his home. He clouded the sky with his smoke so that day was dark as night. He burned their crops, devoured their animals, and his heat caused all the rivers and lakes to dry up."

Maple gulped.

"When Tar came for the city, none could stop him. Their magic and spells just bounced off his charred skin, thick as armor. But when the serpent came for Damavash's home, the young man stepped forward to save his family and the fire gods smiled upon him. A golden eagle, carrying armor in its claws, dropped from the skies and gave Damavash the gift. The magical armor deflected all of the fire Tar spat at him, and Damavash drove him to the heart of the mountain and trapped him in it with a spell. Many believe that the glowing veins and the molten fire that seeps from the mountain come from Tar, still trapped inside."

"It was a lion!"

We all turned to look down the table at the older man with the white beard and tall turban who had interrupted. "It was a lion that brought him the armor, and the recent theft proves it."

I leaned forward and addressed the older gentleman. "Theft?"

He scowled, which pulled his bushy white brows together. "Of Damavash's armor from the Royal Artifacts Museum. It's all anyone can talk about these last couple of weeks. Well, that and the wedding, of course."

The woman beside him nodded, her veil sliding over her shoulders. "Over a dozen witnesses, including royal guards, testified that a lion prowled into the museum, lifted the armor onto its back, and walked right out with it."

My draw dropped. "Really?"

Another man scoffed and folded his thick arms across his thicker stomach. The firelight from the lanterns glittered off the many-pointed star medal at his collar and the various ribbons and medals on his shoulder. "Ov courze not. A lazy guart vas ashleep on za job and got heez buddiez to back heem up and say eet vas za fabled lion, returnt to bestow za armor on za next vorthy hero." He shook his head. "Anyvone who beliefs such rubbish ees oon fool. Oon regular zeef shtole eet, zat ees all."

The young woman next to the older man in the black military uniform pressed her eyes shut and pinched the bridge of her nose.

The turbaned man with the long beard narrowed his eyes. "I am not a fool and it is the truth. I am curator of the museum, and I saw the lion carry the armor out with my own eyes. Even if you doubt my sincerity, how do you explain the other witnesses, then? Or how anyone got past the protective spells?" He slammed a hand on the table and the cutlery rattled. Guess I wasn't the only hangry one.

The older military man leaned forward and waggled his thick grey mustache. "Seemple. Eet vas oon shlimy schifter."

A murmur went up and I bit my lip as I leaned back, trying to catch Sam's eye. Sam, my shifter friend, sat a few people over from me on my left. Annie, beside him, put an arm around his shoulders and gave him a little shake. Thank goodness for Annie, our den mother in the bakery. Sam faced daily discrimination because people who could turn to animals just seemed a little too similar to the monsters, like Tar that had at one time ravaged the kingdoms. Real monsters, not just legends.

However, poor Sam, and other shifters like him, didn't deserve to be hated or feared...*especially* Sam. He was kind and gentle and had shocked everyone when he revealed he'd spent most of his life as a snake and only just recently learned to look and act human. It still showed, but I grinned at his neatly combed hair, plastered to his head, and his tucked-in shirt. He was getting the hang of this being human thing.

The woman with the veil shook her head. "No, sir. It was not a shifter. There were specific spells at the museum to keep them out, anticipating just such a thing. No one can figure out how it happened."

The older man with the medals shook his head, his cheeks glowing bright red. "Vell, eet ees not zuch a mystery to myselv. Zere are alvays veaknesses in security and in shpells."

The man in the turban lifted a brow. "You seem confident in this matter."

"I schoult be. I am ze varden of Carclaustra Prison."

Murmurs and gasps sounded down the table, but the young blonde woman beside him stared down at her hands. She looked like she had a headache. I frowned. Carclaustra was where Pritney and Nate were being held for attempting to kill Hank, Shaday, and their families at the Summer Solstice Festival last year. It was the toughest maximum security prison in the kingdoms.

"My goodness," said the man in the turban. He nodded. "You are the famous Bernhardt Beckham, I take it?"

At my left, Yann grumbled, "Eenfamous ees more like eet."

I frowned. Yann, the big teddy bear of a man who worked in the bakery with me, hardly ever uttered a negative word. This Bernhardt must have quite the reputation.

"Then I bow to your expertise in this matter." The man in the turban ducked his head. "How come you to know our royalty? Or perhaps you are connected on the Water side?" He gestured a long hand towards the high table where Hank and Shaday and their families sat.

Bernhardt clapped a hand on the back of the young woman beside him, which sent her lurching forward. "My daughter, Elke, ees za bosom buddy of za preencess Shaday."

The blonde young woman, Elke, gave a small nod.

"And off course, I vonce trained za Fire Keengdom military een za technique my security officer and I developt."

Beside Elke, a pale man in a black uniform like Bernhardt's bowed his head. "Urs Volker. Pleased as to make your acquaintance."

"Vee are shtayink een our own encampment here, een za desert," Bernhardt continued. His gray mustache twitched with every word. "Elke trusts herself een za palace, but not I." He held up his wine glass to a young woman, who moved her way down the table with wine bottles magically hovering beside her. She stiffened, then poured more red into his glass.

"No," Bernhardt continued. "I have locked up too many feelthy lowlifes from zis kingdom to risk shtayink inside za valls of Calloon. Za vorst of za vorst have come from here." He ticked them off on his fingers. "Murdering schifters, dangerous terrorists—"

I frowned. The servant who refilled his glass had grown still and her eyes larger and larger. As Bernhardt rattled off his list, her eyes flashed, she gritted her teeth, and she twitched her hand, ever so slightly. The magically hovering bottle shifted to the side, just a hair, but enough to miss the glass. Red wine spilled all over the tablecloth and soaked Bernhardt's uniform. He jumped back, as did those around him. Wool rose to assist, but the servant waved him off.

"My apologies." She dipped her head, though her eyes still blazed with some deep emotion—anger, maybe?

Bernhardt rose and threw his stained cloth napkin to the

ground. "Vell. Za service ees not vat it ees een za Air Kingdom." He huffed.

His daughter, Elke, held her hands over the tablecloth
and dried the puddle of red wine. "It's all right," she said
to the young woman who'd spilled. "It was just an
accident."

I frowned. It hadn't looked like an accident to me.
Maybe she hadn't appreciated Bernhardt's insulting
comments toward her people?

The servant bowed and moved away.

"Hmpf. Vell, at least my tent ees nearby. I shall change,
and then return." He bowed and stomped off through the
sand toward the many tents that formed a camp in the
desert valley between the city and the volcano.

As that end of the table gradually resumed their conversation, I turned back to Wool. He raised a dark brow and
lowered his voice. "It was an eagle."

Maple giggled, which seemed to startle her, because she
pressed a hand over her mouth and stifled it. A loud sigh
came from Wiley on her other side, and Wool frowned at
him. I thought quick to come up with some topic that would
be a distraction from the love triangle next to me. Maple
had been stressing for weeks, months really. Not only were
we to make the cake for Hank and Shaday's wedding, our
biggest event to date, but starting tomorrow we'd be working
alongside the Fire Kingdom bakers, including Maple's
crush, Wool. Only problem was, she and Wiley had a thing
going too, and yet she still found the room to worry for me
and my feelings about the wedding. The girl was about to
have a meltdown.

"Uh... so, I think I understand the legend. But what was
that about my snarky little fire being a Damavash flame?"

Wool's face softened. "The Fire Kingdom produces the

best fires, it's well known, and the best of the best come from the Damavash Volcano."

"Hmph." Iggy gave a proud sniff.

"We work with them and train them to be dance fires, hearth fires, battle fires, and cooking and baking fires, like Iggy.

"Wow." I cocked my head to the side. "So, you're from the Fire Kingdom."

"Yeah, where'd you think I was from?" Iggy opened his eyes wide.

"Uh...." To be honest I hadn't considered it before. My heart sunk a little. I guess that made me a pretty bad friend. "I just assumed the Water Kingdom."

"Well you assumed wrong." Iggy folded his arms.

"Attention!"

I looked up. Behind Wool, Amelia stood, her dark, slender arms lifted with her white gauzy dress blowing lazily around her in the breeze. "We will continue the toasts momentarily, *after* dinner is served."

A collective sigh rose up among the guests.

"Thank the sea goddess," I muttered. I was getting good at using Water Kingdom sayings. I nudged Maple and she chuckled, then nodded that yes, she'd noticed.

A magical line of floating dishes snaked its way into the tent. From under the golden covers the scents of juicy lamb, savory spices, and perfumed rice wafted out. I had to gulp to keep from drooling all over the table. And just as the dishes stopped in front of us and the lids began to lift on their own, a tall, beefy young man strode to the center of the tables and stood before the royalty. The lids on the food dishes clattered shut again and I bit my lip to keep from screaming.

He squared his shoulders and stood with his legs wide. "I have something to say."

2

ARIO GRANDE

T he tall, beefy man planted himself in front of the royal table like he owned it and glared at Shaday's father, King Benam. His mane of long black hair flowed over his broad shoulders.

I spoke in Maple's ear. "Middle Eastern Fabio?"

She shrugged back, an apologetic smile on her face. Right. Human thing. The muscles on top of muscles thing wasn't my type, but many women would probably call him handsome. I gasped as I thought of something. "Maple, do you think this could be Shaday's secret lover?"

She cocked her head to the side. "Maybe."

My stomach turned with nerves—was he about to profess his love and make a scene? Maybe they'd call the wedding off. I frowned as I caught myself and shook my head. No. I couldn't even think like that. No point getting my hopes up. Not that I had any hopes. I had reached the acceptance phase of grief, and had *no* hopes, I reminded myself. Right.

Amelia approached him. "Sir, we would be happy to hear your toast, but we'd hate for our esteemed guests to be distracted by their hunger and miss out on anything you have to say, so perhaps...." She gestured to his seat.

Way to go being diplomatic, Amelia. I licked my lips as I eyed the platters of food hovering just out of reach.

He glared at her, his thick black eyebrows hanging low over his small dark eyes. "Do you know who I am?"

Amelia opened her mouth to speak but he cut her off.

"I am Ario Tuk, Prince of the Reydeen, fiercest of the Fire Kingdom tribes." He pounded a fist to his chest, a thick pelt of hair revealed by the plunging neckline on his robes.

"I'm still going to call him Fabio in my head," I muttered.

"No one knows what you're talking about." Iggy rolled his eyes.

Amelia cast a glance at Shaday, whose expression stayed as placid as ever, but her dark eyes blazed. Amelia stepped closer to Ario and attempted to usher him back to his seat with her arms outstretched. "Well, Ario, we're honored to have you join us, but if you'll just wait a moment for dinner to be served—"

Ario pushed past her toward the royal table, shoulder checking her on the way. Amelia stumbled back.

"Hey!" Wiley pushed back from the table, but Maple put a hand on his arm and shook her head.

"We're not at home," she hissed.

Wiley huffed and slowly lowered, his eyes blazing at Ario, who hadn't even noticed.

I balled my hands into fists. My palms burned where my nails dug into them. "I say let Wiley pummel him."

Maple raised her brows at me and leaned close to whisper in my ear. "Look at his arms! They're as big around as Wiley's waist. You tell me who'd do the pummeling." She glared at Ario. "Though he deserves to be taught a thing or two about manners."

She was right, of course. The man was massive... and rude.

Ario swept into a shallow bow, though he kept his smirking face lifted to the king's. He straightened and sniffed. "King Benam, on behalf of the Reydeen Tribe, we wish to express our thanks for your invitation to your daughter's wedding. Though, of course, we had hoped we might be sitting there beside you, with one of our own as the groom in place of this pale foreigner." He sneered in Hank's direction.

Surprised murmurs echoed from the guests.

I gritted my teeth. "That's my pale foreigner you're talking about."

Behind Hank, Francis hissed and bared his teeth like a cat.

"Mmm." I glanced down the row at Rhonda. She fanned herself. "I love it when he does that."

Shaday lifted her chin. "Ario. You presented your suit, and I declined it. Several times. Show some good grace and return to your seat."

Oh shoot, Shaday. Her father, a thin man with a long white beard, cleared his throat and shifted in his seat.

Ario's full lips curled and he addressed the king. "One of your women is speaking out of turn. All the more evidence that you should have married her to someone like me, who would have kept her in check with a strong hand." He glared at Shaday. "If you'd chosen me you could have been a queen."

My jaw dropped. What a jerk.

Hank cleared his throat and stood. "I won't deny that I am both in need of a tan and am in many ways woefully ignorant of your culture. That's something I hope Shaday's influence will help to remedy. However, I am not so ignorant as to think that a woman speaking on her own behalf is out of turn. What is out of turn, is interrupting someone else's engagement feast by forcefully shoving oneself between hundreds of guests and their delicious-smelling food."

"Here here," Annie muttered.

Ario glared at Hank, and though Hank kept his smile pleasant, his eyes burned.

Shaday called a guard over to her, whispered something to him behind her hand, and he left. In moments, several other guards appeared at Ario's sides. He shrugged them away, but was escorted back to his seat.

Amelia huffed, smoothed her dress, and then stood again in the center of the square. "Finally, dinner is served."

Guests clapped their appreciation as silver and gold lids floated off platters and dishes. I groaned in happiness as I lifted a flat oval of naan smothered in garlic and butter. I ripped Maple half and put it on her plate, then reached for some rice.

But as I looked up, I glanced toward the royal table. I'd really been trying not to, but like a train wreck, I couldn't look away. Shaday leaned over to Hank and whispered something. I cocked my head. What had she said? He smiled warmly at her, his blue eyes glittering. I frowned. She leaned over and pressed her lips to his cheek. My heartbeat thundered in my ears and chills crept up my neck. His hand slid across the tablecloth and covered hers.

CRACK!

Hank's eyes lifted to mine as the sharp noise of splintering glass split the air. His eyes widened and he pulled back his hand. I jerked back as my champagne flute split and glass fell onto my plate. My chest heaved. I'd done that. I hadn't meant to, but I'd shattered that glass out of anger and surprise and hurt. Maple turned to me with wide eyes.

"Ooh my," Yann muttered.

Before anyone could say anything else, I pushed back from the low table, unfolded my aching legs, and stood. I threw down my silk napkin and muttered, "I have to use the restroom," to no one in particular, then stalked off before anyone could stop me.

My hands trembled at my sides. I didn't dare to look back at Hank to check his reaction, but I wondered if he'd come after me. I sighed, disgusted with myself. At his own wedding feast? Nope, he wasn't coming after me, because he belonged at his fiancée's side, and I belonged—well, pretty much anywhere but at that table. I stomped away from the low tables, the bustling wait staff, and the billowing gauzy fabric that formed a loose canopy above the feast. My feet sank into the sand of the desert and I wrapped my arms around my bare arms, goose bumps prickling my skin. Musicians had begun to perform, and the high trilling notes of a flute floated across the cool breeze, growing quieter as I stomped away. I glanced back and caught sight of several fire dancers sweeping into the space between the tables. They held flames in their palms and their skirts trailed behind them. I huffed. Did everything here have to be so exotic and perfect?

I knew Hank was marrying Shaday, so why was I so upset? I let out a shaky exhale. It had been that kiss on the cheek, the touch of the hand. Those were intimate things. Things you did with someone you liked and cared about. Even if he didn't love her, and she didn't love him, they had affection for each other. And with marriage and time together, that might deepen into something more. Something that left no room for me.

I skirted a peaked teal tent with gold trim, and once I stood out of sight of guests and wait staff, buried my face in my hands. *I'm fine, I'm fine with this, I knew it was coming, we're all adults, it's just a formality.* It had almost become a mantra, I'd told myself these words so many times over the last few months. I should have had them printed on an inspirational poster and hung it on the wall of my room in the palace.

I forced my shallow breaths to come a little deeper, but my lungs felt tight and my heart pounded. On the airship over, Wiley had told me he'd been reading self-help books to better himself. I translated that as being "to have a chance with Maple," but whatever his motivation, it was commendable. He'd told me about a relaxation technique that focused on noticing the sounds, smells, and sensations around you to "ground yourself." As we were hundreds of feet above the ground at the time, and my anxiety at that moment stemmed from floating through the air in a giant balloon, noticing my surroundings hadn't been the most helpful.

I pressed a hand to my aching chest and gulped. Now might be a good time to try it though, since my feet were planted firmly in the warm desert sand.

I closed my eyes and listened. The haunting, reedy flute music filled the night air, with the murmur of conversation and the clinks of cutlery from the feast humming below it. I listened more. Next came water, lapping water, from the small oasis dotted with palms nearby, where camels grunted and slurped water. I let out a shaky breath and relaxed a little. The desert breeze blew curled tendrils of my hair across my nape and sent the tents flapping.

"Vee both know sees eesn't za real reason you vant to schpeak vis mee."

My eyes flew open. I knew that voice. It belonged to Bernhardt Beckham, the warden of Carclaustra.

"You're delusional."

I bit my lip. I didn't recognize the woman's voice. I crept forward; the soft sand beneath my sandaled feet kept my steps quiet. I peered around the side of the tent.

In front of another tent that glowed from within stood Bernhardt Beckham, the warden of infamous Carclaustra prison, speaking with a dark-haired woman. I crept closer, still hidden behind the fabric of the tent. Bernhardt buttoned a black jacket trimmed in silver—he must've have changed after that waitress spilled on him. He refastened the star medal at his collar.

"Come now, Maddie—"

She jabbed at him, her face tight and pale. "Don't you dare call me that. It's Ms. L'Orange to you."

"Psh." He stepped closer and she backed away. "Vee are not schtrangers and I vill not address you az vone."

The woman's hair and the scarf tied around her neck blew in the breeze, silhouetted against the glowing tent. "I want them. You have no right to have them."

"Zey are just az much mine az yours, Maddie."

She raised her voice. "You had no right! I'm writing that piece, and you can't stop me."

Bernhardt shrugged. "Vell, zen you von't mind eef zey find zer way to ze press. Oh vait, you are ze press. Vell, I'm sure your colleagues vill be happy to have some scandalous news to report on, yes? Zough I am afraid eet might ruin your reputation."

She raised her hand and I gasped as she swung at his face. But Bernhardt moved quicker than I would have guessed possible and caught her wrist before her slap could land.

"Ah, Maddie. You zee? I am vone schtep ahead of you —alvays."

The woman yanked her arm back. "You're going to

answer for your crimes. I'll make sure of it." She turned, her dark hair blowing around her, and stalked off. Bernhardt chuckled and turned to the tent behind him. He waved a hand and a shimmering bubble flashed around the whole thing, then disappeared. He'd cast some sort of spell. A waiter approached, dressed in billowing white robes like all the others, and held a round tray up to him.

"Sir, a drink? Also, I believe your colleague is searching for you."

Bernhardt plucked up a champagne flute and nodded at the servant. "Urs? I'll be right along, zen." He walked toward the party as if nothing had happened. What could he have that would ruin that woman, Ms. L'Orange's reputation? And was he blackmailing her? As the head of a prison, that seemed pretty shady to me.

As the servant turned to follow, he faced in my direction for the briefest of moments. That face. I knew that face. My breath caught. Horace. He smirked, and I gasped as he disappeared out of sight behind the tent. Had I imagined it? For months now I'd been thinking up ways to contact him, ever since I learned he was my brother.

I lurched forward, following around the curve of the tent. I'd thought of sending up the Badlands Army signal, but it'd be too public and I'd probably end up arrested. I stumbled in the sand and pressed a hand to the snapping canvas of the tent at my side. I walked quicker so as not to lose him. I'd even thought of visiting Nate and Pritney in prison. They'd know how to contact Horace, but the thought of contacting two people who had tried to kill me turned my stomach. And now Horace showed up here, of all places? Heart pounding, I jogged forward, my feet twisting in the sand.

"Imogen?"

I screamed as a strong hand closed around my wrist from behind.

I whirled to find Hank looking as panicked as I felt. I let out a heavy sigh and pressed my eyes closed. I smiled. "Hank."

"Are you all right? What are you doing back here?"

I half-turned, part of me still longing to follow Horace. But what if I was wrong? Maybe the lack of food, surplus of alcohol, and intense stress had my eyes playing tricks on me. Mirages were a desert thing, right? They probably didn't happen in the middle of the night, but who knew?

"What's wrong? Are you looking for someone?"

I turned to face Hank fully. "Don't freak out, but I thought I saw Horace."

Hank paled and a muscle jumped in his cheek. "Are you all right? Did he threaten you?" He turned his head and called over his shoulder. "Francis!"

A slight breeze blew the tendrils of hair at my neck. I turned and found Francis hovering directly behind me, breathing on my neck. "Gah!" I jumped.

He lifted a dark brow. "You rang."

"Imogen saw Horace here, at the feast. I need you to look for him and alert security."

I held up my hands. "Look, I could be wrong. I haven't eaten in hours and have had a few glasses of wine."

Hank ignored me. "Please, Francis."

The vampire shrugged his narrow shoulders. "Your father ordered me to keep a close watch on you."

"I'm sorry, I know it isn't fair for you to have to do this." Hank nodded. "But finding Horace is more important. I'll answer to my father if he takes issue with it."

"Very well. And in any case, I don't mind being your bodyguard. You're the only member of your family I've ever been able to stand. And I've served three generations of them." Francis swept away as silently as he'd arrived.

Hank wrung one hand around his other wrist, bunching up the gold cuffs of his uniform. He looked away and shrugged his broad shoulders. "Were you—Did you come out here to speak with Horace?"

I sighed. "I—I just needed some air." I lifted a finger. "But we've talked about this. He's my brother."

Hank held up his big hands. "Imogen. Someone might hear."

I huffed, but lowered my voice. "Sorry. I know he's a wanted criminal and all that, but... I just want the chance to talk to him."

Hank crossed his muscled arms. "Fine. Once he's behind bars."

I shook my head. "He saved me as a baby, and he led us to Wee Ferngroveshire so I could learn that. He won't hurt me... probably."

Hank threw his head back and looked at the stars, exposing his throat. As frustrated as I was, I longed to kiss it. He leveled his gaze at me. "I'm not okay with 'probably.' 'Probably,' isn't good enough when we're talking about your safety."

"You don't get to decide."

He looked pained. "I know I don't." His nostrils flared. "But if *you're* not going to value your life, I'd hope you'd think about how much I value it, before you go risking everything to—" He lowered his voice. "To speak to your homicidal brother."

I set my jaw. "I care what you think, I don't want to hurt you, but he's the only brother I've got and I want to know who he is."

Hank let out a heavy sigh and I crossed my arms. I toed

the sand and willed my breathing deeper, breath after breath. Finally my chest relaxed a little. I lifted a palm and looked at Hank. "What are you doing?" I tried for a smile. "It's your wedding feast—they might notice you're missing."

"I don't care. We need to talk." He sighed and lifted his brows in the middle. "And I don't want to fight."

My eyes darted to his, then dropped again. I kicked the sand. "About what?" I didn't wait for him to answer. "I'm sure it can wait."

He stepped closer. "You've been saying that for weeks. Imogen, I love you. I know this is hard for me—it must be terrible for you. I want to know what you're thinking, how you're feeling."

I stepped back and only lifted my eyes as high as his chest. "I'm thinking that you're getting married to someone who isn't me and that's not ideal, but it's happening. Like, in a few days happening. And yeah, I'll have to deal with it." I gave a jerky shrug. "And I'm *thinking* this, us talking in the dark under the stars, doesn't look good, so we should get back to the feast."

I turned to leave.

"Imogen, wait."

I turned and lifted my brows, my lips pressed into a tight line.

"I saw you break that glass."

My face darkened. "It was an accident."

"Because you're upset—understandably. I am, too." He licked his lips. "When I was younger, before my father found my tutor and I learned to control my powers, I'd have, well, outbursts when I was stressed or upset." He stepped closer and reached for my hand. Just like he'd reached for Shaday's.

My nostrils flared. "Well, you didn't look that upset earlier. And besides, I'm fine, it was just an accident."

His brows pinched together in confusion. I let out a shaky breath. I was letting him see how upset I was. I needed to reel it in. I needed to not be upset, because it would be a waste—I saw no point in fighting something inevitable. I pressed my eyes closed and when I opened them again, arranged my face to be pleasant and calm, though my chest still felt choked.

"Come on. It's your party and *you* can cry if *you* want to, but I'm heading back for some shish kebabs." I flashed a tight smile and headed back to the feast and the music and the fire dancers before he could stop me. Hank called after me, but I didn't turn back.

3

TOO MANY COOKS

We spent the night glamping in tents out in the desert, and the next morning rode camels into the walled city of Calloon, the capital of the Fire Kingdom. The other bakers and I shuffled through narrow, winding streets, following Wool to the main square and then to the royal riad.

K'ree and Wool acted as tour guides, pointing out the best spots for a mint tea (which was every other cafe, apparently), scoffing at the vendors selling knockoff Damavash flames (I already had a genuine one, thank you very much) and identifying the various piles of spices and exotic fruits we passed. I found all the distractions such a welcome relief from agonizing over my wreck of a love life that I actually forgot to be depressed and had some real fun.

When we passed through the doors of the riad and entered the center courtyard with its rectangular fountain pool, bordered on all sides by two-story balconies, it felt as though we'd entered a different world. Instead of shouting merchants hawking their wares, birds chirped as they flitted about the garden and we got some relief from the heat inside the shaded space. Wool led us through the tiled courtyard, down a winding hall lined with archways, and finally into the back of the palace to the kitchen.

After we met the other five Fire bakers, Wool gave us an orientation. Recessed shelves lined one entire white plaster wall. Wool gestured at various bottles, translating the labels for us.

"We'll cast a translation spell, of course," he assured Maple, and the little line between her brows relaxed.

She pressed a hand to her chest. "Thank goodness—I was feeling a bit worried I'd use long pepper." She gestured at one glass jar. "When I meant to use regular black pepper." She nodded at another.

Wool chuckled. "No worries, Maple." He placed a hand on her shoulder and guided us on to the next wall. Beside me, Wiley sucked in a deep, loud breath through his nose and blew it out. Again, and again. I gave him a side-eye look.

"You okay there?"

He lifted a brow. "Hm? Oh, yeah." He sniffed in again as we shuffled past one of the large tiled islands that occupied the center of the kitchen.

"Really? Because you seem like you're about to hyper-ventilate and pass out."

He shook his head and blew out a stream of air with an open mouth. "Nah. Just this breathing technique I've been reading about. It's supposed to help with relaxation."

"Well, you're not doing it right, because it's stressing me out."

He rolled his eyes, but muttered, "Sorry. It's just *this* guy—"

"Wool?"

"Yeah, whatever. It's like he thinks he knows everything.

I've been baking for plenty of years, buddy, thank you very much, am I right?"

I lifted a brow and blew my bangs out of my eyes. "I had no idea what any of those spices were."

Wiley's eyes fell to his shoes. "Yeah. Me neither."

Wool pointed out the stove, where they kept the pans and baking sheets in the various black cupboards that matched the black-and-white-patterned floor tiles, and showed us to the recessed ovens that they'd cleared to make room for our flames. I spent a few minutes placing Iggy in one and getting him settled in with a supply of split logs. Wool and Maple moved to a corner to speak more.

Iggy looked past my shoulder toward him. "You think he liked my joke? He smiled and I think he chuckled a little."

I stacked some logs to the side of the oven and lifted a brow. "Who?"

The little flame rolled his eyes. "Wool, of course. Who else?"

I tugged my lips to the side and tried to suppress my smile. "Well, of course, how silly of me. What joke again?"

Iggy grabbed a log and pulled it closer, absentmindedly munching on the end of it. A tendril of steam rose from the wood. "You know, just a minute ago. Someone mentioned the toasts from last night and I said, 'I make toasts every morning—for the king's breakfast. He likes his with butter and grape jelly.' You didn't hear?"

I chuckled. "Right, that joke. Hilarious."

Iggy sniffed. "You're just jealous that Wool likes me better."

I opened my mouth in an exaggerated O. "If I didn't know better, I'd say somebody had a crush."

Iggy dropped the log and looked offended. "Oh, because I can't just appreciate a suave and cultured man who appreciates *me* as a friend? Way to act real insecure Imogen, real insecure."

I placed the last logs inside the oven and raised my palms. "My apologies. I'll attempt to be less threatened."

Grinning, I joined the others in a circle up around Wool and Maple.

Maple folded her hands across her apron. "This afternoon, the royal families are having a tea together." She glanced up at Wool. "We thought it'd be fun for the Water Kingdom bakers to make one of our specialties for the Fire Kingdom royalty."

"And we'll make one of our dishes for Hank and his family," Wool finished in his deep voice.

"So... what are we making?" Annie asked.

Maple took a deep breath. "Macaroons, but with a Fire Kingdom twist. We'll infuse one batch with rose water, and for the other we'll use pistachio instead of almond flour."

I grinned. "Yum."

Sam wrung his hands. "Tricky though, macaroons."

I nodded. This was true, and we had foreign royalty to impress.

Wool flashed his white smile. "And we'll be making shortbread cookies."

Wiley scoffed and muttered, "How original."

"The pastry will be perfumed with orange blossom water and filled with a date jelly spiced with nutmeg." Wool nodded.

Wiley crossed his arms. "Okay, that's actually pretty original."

Wool spread his arms wide. "Our kitchen is your kitchen. Make yourselves at home, and if we can help in any way, do not hesitate to ask." Wool winked at Maple and her cheeks flushed bright pink. Wiley scowled and slammed a gold metal mixing bowl down on the counter, which made the rest of us jump. K'ree and I flashed eyes at each other. This was going to be an interesting day.

We Water bakers moved to one side of the kitchen and gathered around a tile-topped island, while the Fire bakers moved to the other side. Maple delegated out tasks and within minutes the kitchen bustled with all of us moving about in the relatively tight space. After the enchanted mortars and pestles had ground the bowls of almonds fine enough, I stood beside Maple and sifted the almond flour and sugar mixture through a sieve, as she did the same with the pistachio flour mixture.

I bumped my shoulder against hers. "So, how's your Bermuda love triangle going?"

She grinned. "I don't know what you're saying."

I glanced over my shoulder and spotted Wool laughing with a bunch of his bakers. "I think you do." I waggled my brows at her.

A pink flush rose from her neck and spread over her cheeks. She turned the mixing bowl into the sieve and started over to catch more clumps. She lowered her voice so that only I could hear over the clanks of pans and whir of spoons in bowls.

"Ugh. I'm so worried about it. I mean, I like Wool, but I also like Wiley." She shook the sieve harder, more fine powder trailing into the mixing bowl below. "And I'm trying to be professional. This is our first collaboration with royal bakers from another kingdom. Everything has to go perfectly." A little crease formed between her brows. "And if Wiley gets upset and starts acting like a child, or he offends Wool and they kick us out of the kitchen, what am I—"

I laughed and put a hand on her shoulder. "That's not going to happen. Everything will be wonderful. Trust me."

She looked up and let out a little sigh. "Oh Imogen, I hope so."

I smiled back. "It will. I mean, rose and pistachio macaroons? A brilliant idea, who wouldn't love them?"

She nodded. "I hope Shaday and her family do."

"They will."

As I put my flour through a third and final pass, just to be extra diligent, I wiped the back of my hand across my brow. My bangs stuck to my forehead and I blew out a little breath. "Man, it is warm in here though."

Sam, standing across the kitchen island from me, closed his milky blue eyes behind his thick glasses. "Mm. It'sss perfect."

I grinned. Maybe being a snake shifter left him a bit cold-blooded when in human form.

K'ree stood behind several mixing bowls, supervising the spelled wooden spoons that beat eggs whites and sugar together until they formed peaks. "If they'd put the kitchen in the central courtyard we'd get more of a breeze," she grumbled. She blew her gauzy black veil out of her face as she leaned over to the check on her mixture. "That's how my family's home is set up. But here at the back of the house, all the windows face the back alley."

I glanced up. The windows had all been opened, but not much air flowed through. I used my apron to dab at my neck. When K'ree gave me the signal, I sifted my flour mixture over the egg whites she'd been working on. Then I moved to the Fire Kingdom side of the room. One of the women hummed a spell to make her spoons whirl round a bowl. The intoxicating aroma of orange blossoms wafted up and I took a deep inhale. It reminded me of a warm spring day. I opened my eyes and tapped Wool on the shoulder.

He turned. "Yes, Imogen? How can I help?"

I pointed at the shelves of spices. "Do you have beetroot powder?"

He grinned. "Of course."

Wool scanned the labels and then plucked a glass jar of intense fuchsia powder and handed it to me.

I held it up to the light and peered at it. "Thank you, Wool. I probably would have grabbed the saffron if left to my own devices." The bright red spice looked similar to the beetroot in the shadowed recess of the shelves.

Wool smiled. "That would make for... interesting macaroons."

"Inedible is more like it." I lifted the jar. "Thanks again, *and* for hosting us in your kitchen. I know there's a lot of us."

"More make merrier." He ducked his tall head and as I moved to return to my work station, I caught both Maple and Wiley watching before they whirled around and stared down at their work. I chuckled to myself and stood beside Maple again.

"Yes, he's still just as charming as ten minutes ago, if you were wondering."

K'ree chuckled and Wiley made a point of banging his spoon loudly against the side of the metal mixing bowl as he beat the butter and sugar together for the filling. *Real mature, Wiley.*

I added a couple of spoonfuls of the beetroot to my mixture, then used a spatula to fold it all together. Gradually the batter took on a bright pink hue. I rolled my eyes at myself as I scraped and turned the bowl. Not like I could judge Wiley. Hank had tried to talk to me last night and I'd acted like a child. I scraped and folded the batter again. I'd overreacted... probably. I mean, he had touched her hand and she'd given him a kiss on the cheek. That went beyond acquaintances—heck, I didn't even kiss my friends on the cheek. Then again, this was another culture and maybe that was normal. I frowned. Shaday, while beautiful and composed, had never struck me as the touchy-feely type.

I jerked when Maple placed a hand on my arm.

"Oh!" I shook my head to clear it. "Sorry, kinda zoned out there for a moment."

She nodded, a little crease between her blonde brows. "Yeah... you seemed somewhere else for a moment. Just wanted to make sure you didn't overstir it."

"Thank you." I meant it. It was easy to do, even when you were fully paying attention. I lifted the spatula and let a ribbon of the pink batter drip back into the bowl and then counted to ten. By the count of nine, the ribbon had fully reabsorbed into the batter.

"You stopped me just in time—any more and I would have overdone it." I bumped Maple's shoulder. "And that's why you're the boss."

She grinned, but swatted away the compliment. I piped the macaroon mixture into circles on a baking sheet, tapped the sheet on the tiled counter a few times to loosen any air bubbles, and then set out the tray to dry. In this dry heat, it wouldn't take long. In the meantime, I helped mix and pour Maple's batch of the pistachio cookies. Though I tried to keep my focus, my mind kept drifting to my anger the night before—the way I'd broken that glass. I hoped I could keep my cool during the wedding, which loomed only two days away.

Wiley brushed past me and plucked up a tray of dried green macaroon cookies, their tops shiny and glossy. "You've got that thundercloud look on your face again."

I straightened up and licked my lips. "I'm fine." I thought about it. "Did I really look upset?"

Wiley raised his brows. "I wouldn't want to be on the receiving end of that look, I'll tell you that."

I sighed. Maybe my resolution to stay focused on baking wasn't going as smoothly as I'd hoped.

"You could try that breathing technique I mentioned." He held the tray at chest height and waited for me to answer.

I spun around and grabbed a tray of pink cookies, ready for the oven. We walked to the wall dotted with ovens and hot with baking fires already blazing. Several of the other bakers stood there, checking their bakes or placing in new batches.

I scoffed. "Yeah, 'cause that's working so well for you, Mr. Zen."

"Sorry to interrupt." Wool turned from the wall of ovens and Wiley muttered, "Great, here we go."

I ignored his comment as I slid the tray of cookies to Iggy. "When you're halfway through I'll take the cover off and let the steam out."

"No!" Iggy opened his mouth wide. "C'mon, I want to hear this."

I grinned. "Sorry." I placed the wooden cover over the oven, which muffled Iggy's grumblings.

"Did I overhear you discussing the Mendel breathing technique?" Wool lifted a dark brow.

Wiley crossed his arms over his chest, but cocked his head to the side. "You know it?"

Wool flashed his bright smile. "Yeah. I got really into it about a year ago. Helped me during some stressful times."

"Uh, yeah." Wiley shifted to face him more fully. "That's uh—that's what I'm using it for." He rubbed the back of his neck. "I can get a little hotheaded sometimes."

"I think we all can."

I pictured the glass shattering last night and nodded my agreement.

"But when I started here after the competition last year, the Mendel breath was difficult—I'll be honest, *embarrassing* —to use in the kitchen. I mean, people constantly asked me if I was hyperventilating." Wool flashed a bright smile, then lowered his voice. Wiley and I leaned closer to catch his words. "Mena over there was terrified of me. She thought I was about to have a meltdown every time I did the breath. Of course, she only told me this *later*." He grinned.

I smiled back. "So... what do you do instead?"

Wool lifted his palms. "Something easier, and quieter. Four square breath. Try it. I'll talk you through it."

My eyes slid to Wiley. He licked his lips, then gave a tight nod.

"All right." Wool smiled and rubbed his hands together. "Close your eyes."

"Has anyone punched the other one yet?" Iggy yelled through the oven cover.

I peeled an eye open and hissed, "Shush. We're trying a breathing technique."

"Oh. And then they're going to fight?"

I ignored my flame and closed my eyes again.

"Take a deep breath," Wool coached in his soothing, velvety voice. "Hold it for a count of one, two, three, four, then let it out to a count of four. Pause again, and then take a deep breath for four." He talked us through a few rounds.

"There. Do you feel better?"

I opened my eyes and blinked, dazzled by the brightness in the kitchen. I smiled. "I do. I feel like I can take my first deep breath in days." I bit my lip and looked towards my friend. "Wiley?"

He looked as though he'd just woken up, his lids half closed. "Your voice is so relaxing."

Wool chuckled. "I get that a lot."

Wiley blinked, then sighed. "I'll use that one again. Hey, thanks, man."

Wool clapped him on the shoulder. "Of course." They walked away together. "Have you tried meditation? That was another for me that really...."

I shook my head, marveling at Wiley getting along with his rival for Maple's affection. "This world never ceases to amaze me."

"It's quiet out there. Are they dead?"

I rolled my eyes, but plucked the cover off Iggy's oven. Steam poured out. At home, I would have closed my eyes and savored the moist heat. Here in the desert though, I just felt like I was wilting.

"We're going to leave the cover off for the last half of the bake," I informed him. Then I leaned closer and whispered, "No, it's even crazier than if they fought—they're actually getting along."

Iggy's mouth gaped open. "What?" He skirted to the side and looked past me. I followed his gaze to where Wiley and Wool stood together, laughing to the point of having to wipe tears from their eyes. Maple turned toward me, the whites showing all around her eyes, and shook her head. I shrugged at her. I had no idea how that had happened.

When Iggy finished the bake, I carried the tray back to the workstation and plunked it down in front of Maple. She stood folded over, her head resting in her hand, with her elbow on the counter. She shook her head slowly as she watched Wiley and Wool chanting a baking song together.

"They're besties now, look at them."

I sank down beside her and leaned my head against hers.

"They've completely forgotten about me." Her voice was full of wonder.

"Well." I sighed. "At least you don't have to worry about them fighting over you anymore."

"I suppose that's a good thing." She nibbled her fingernail.

Once the cookies cooled, Wiley, Yann, and Annie piped the rose-flavored buttercream filling in, and then topped it with another cookie, making a little sandwich.

Maple grinned. "All right, who wants to do the taste test?"

"I luf macaroons!" Yann raised his hand and Maple nodded. The two of them plucked up a macaroon each, Yann a pink one pistachio one and Maple one of the green pistachio-flavored cookies. They touched them together.

"Cheers," Maple said, before taking a delicate bite. She closed her eyes and moaned. "Yum."

Yann threw the whole thing into his mouth. He'd chosen cookies from my batch, so I watched his face to gauge his reaction and hoped they'd turned out. One eye fluttered closed, while his lips twisted to the side. He turned quickly and spat the cookie into his hand. My mouth fell open.

"What's wrong?"

"Ugh. Dey are, how you say, like lemon?" Yann downed the glass of milk that Annie conjured up for him.

"Sour?" I gasped. "How could they have come out sour?" Maybe the rose water had done something unusual to the filling? I plucked up a cookie and nibbled the edge, then immediately spat it out into my hand. "They *are* sour—the cookie itself. How?" I shook my head. "These were from my batch."

K'ree plucked up another pink one from a bowl Sam had mixed and shook her head. "This one's delicious."

Maple ran her hands through her hair. "We won't have enough. We have to figure out what went wrong and all work together to get another batch done. It'll look terrible if we run out of them. Tea's in half an hour, so we can serve some while we make more, and restock their plates."

I stared at the partly eaten pink macaroon in my hand. "So only mine are bad?" I went back in my head. "I used the right amount of flour and sifted it well. I even did an extra pass through the sieve. And even though I got distracted for a minute there, the ribbon test meant I stopped at the right time. I didn't add anything unusual except the beetroot for coloring."

Annie shook her head at the jar of fuchsia powder. "That wouldn't have made them taste badly."

Maple slid up to me and gave me a careful look. "Imogen. What were you thinking about when you were mixing and got distracted?"

"She had that 'I'm going to murder someone' look on her face." Wiley folded his arms.

"I was thinking about last night." I bit my lip.

"You got really upset last night." Maple grabbed my upper arms and gave them a little squeeze. "Remember in the competition when you made Rhonda and Francis kiss—before they were together?"

"You matchmaker, you." Annie winked at me.

"It was because you'd accidentally poured your feelings into the bake, remember?" Maple grimaced.

I nodded, my stomach sinking.

"I think that may have happened again today."

I sighed. "You're right. You have to be." I looked around at my friends. "I'm so sorry, everyone. I'll do better this next time. I'll work on them so no one has to do double and then—"

Maple grimaced and I stopped short. "What?"

She took a deep breath. "Don't be mad."

"Oh geez, what?" I slumped.

"I think it'd be best if you took a break from the kitchen for the rest of today."

I shook my head.

"You're stressed—understandably. Why don't you take a breather? Explore the riad?" Maple's big eyes pleaded with me.

"I can be more useful here." I folded my arms. I'd go crazy if I had to sit around sweating in my rooms and twiddle my thumbs, with nothing to think about but the wedding.

"I hate this as much as you do." Maple squeezed my arms again. "You're my best friend. But I don't think you're feeling your best today—take a break?" She winced. "Please don't hate me."

I rolled my eyes. "Agh. Geez." I grabbed her wrists. "You're the sweetest person in the world, how could I hate you?"

She pouted.

I slumped and my eyes dropped, ready to accept defeat. Then I spotted a little roll of paper in Maple's apron pocket. She'd been making a list earlier of items she wanted from the marketplace here in Calloon. I snatched the scroll. "Fine. I'll stay out of the kitchen, but I'm still going to make myself useful. I'll go to the market and get what you wanted."

Her eyes grew round. "By yourself?"

I untied my apron and yanked it over my head. It got caught on my bun and I twisted to extricate myself.

"Imogen." She moved closer and lowered her voice. "You

don't know your way around. And you're not the best at directions...."

"Wow." I folded my arms. "The compliments just keep coming."

I grinned as she grew flustered, a flush creeping up her neck. "I didn't— No, I meant—" She huffed. "It's not the safest city and you don't know your way around it. what if you wander into the wrong part of town? Or get kidnapped?" Her mouth formed a little O. She sucked in air. "Or what if Horace finds you. You said you thought you saw him last night."

I shook the scroll and grinned at her. "I'll be fine, I'm a big girl. And my eyes were probably playing tricks on me, but he wouldn't hurt me anyway." I walked toward the door, my steps quick. I kept the grin plastered to my face.

"We'll missss you, Imogen." I glanced back. Sam blinked at me, his shoulders slumped.

I chuckled. "Aw, Sam, I'll be back before you know it."

Maple clasped her hands together. "Oh. At least see if Francis will go with you?"

I smiled and waved and wished everyone luck and stepped out into the arched hallway, where I buried my face in my hands and let the tears flow.

I was a mess, an absolute mess of a witch. I'd let my emotions get the best of me last night and broken a glass and had a fight with Hank, and now I'd ruined a bake and been banished from working alongside my friends in the kitchen. I was the worst. The absolute worst.

I used the back of my hand to wipe the tears from my face and dragged my feet down the hallway, passing several closed doors. I headed right, then left, then up a staircase we definitely hadn't taken on our way to the kitchen, back down a ramp and finally found myself in another hallway, dotted with potted palms and hanging rugs. I sighed. Just like me to get lost, too. I hadn't seen a single person since leaving the kitchen, but I'd heard voices behind some of the doors. Maybe someone would find and help me if I just started screaming?

I groaned and leaned my shoulder against the hanging rug to my right. Only, I kept leaning and leaning. My stomach lurched as I tumbled through the hidden opening behind the rug and fell into darkness.

4

IN THE BROOM CLOSET

"Ah!" I tripped over my own feet and fell hard on my hip. I sat in near darkness and blew my bangs out of my eyes. "Ow."

"Did you hear something?"

"Besides your terrible singing?"

"Be nice to me or I'll sing louder."

"You wouldn't dare."

The female voices sounded nearby, and one seemed familiar. I stifled a groan and rolled onto my hands and knees on the gritty tiled floor. This part of the palace hadn't been cleaned in a while. Then again, I seemed to be in a hidden room so maybe no one even knew it was here. I stood slowly, my hip aching, and dusted my hands off on my skinny jeans. Then I straightened up and looked around.

My eyes quickly adjusted to the dimness of the closet-sized room. Behind me hung the rug, but in front of me a wooden screen let in some light through its lace-like pattern. Behind it, figures moved and light blazed in orange streaks. I stepped closer and peered through one of the openings.

Shaday, or rather five Shadays, spun in unison, fire trailing from their hands, then they all dropped into a crouch. My mouth fell open—not only at the number of the princess I saw, but at the way they all moved. It was like a dance, but also a fight, with all five moving in perfect timing together.

They spun, leapt, kicked, and flipped, fire whirling around them. Chills crept up my arms and neck, as she— well *they*—danced to a high voice humming some exotic, sliding tune that echoed off the tall ceiling.

I spotted the singer, a curvy blonde girl who stood in the corner against a table draped in a white canvas tarp. Tarps and stacked furniture lined the walls, as if they'd pushed them out of the way to make room for Shaday's martial arts-like dance. I sniffed as I realized why the girl looked famil-iar. She was Elke, Bernhardt's daughter, who'd looked so uncomfortable at the feast the night before.

Shaday did a backflip and dropped immediately into the splits, her soft boots scuffing across the tiled floor. She stayed there, arms lifted overhead with a rope of fire stretched between her hands, and panted. Her chest heaved with her breath. Then her fire and the doppelgangers disap-peared, leaving only one Shaday, who rolled over and lay on the patterned tile floor, spread eagle. I resisted the urge to break into applause. Not only had that been the most impressive display of athleticism I'd ever seen, but from Shaday? Who knew she could move? Who knew she could do anything besides float into rooms in gorgeous gowns and raise an elegant eyebrow now and then in a rare show of emotion.

Elke walked forward, staring at a stopwatch in her hand. "Best time yet—three minutes and forty-five seconds. Did you get burned?"

Shaday, her chest still heaving, propped up on an elbow and watched Elke approach. She peeled some tan gloves that reminded me of pantyhose off her arms and tossed them to the blonde girl. The lacy tattoos on her left hand became visible. Elke caught the gloves and looked them over.

"No. They held up until the last moment. The gloves probably would have gone even longer, but I ran out of steam."

Elke sank down and sat cross-legged beside Shaday, still looking the gloves over. She smiled. "Not bad, huh? Next time I'll enchant them with a longevity spell not just for fire endurance, but for the wearer, too. With the multiplier spell you *are* burning through your magic five times faster, you know? But you're getting better. It looked really impressive."

Shaday grinned up at her and my heart nearly stopped. As crazy a feat as I had just seen her perform, an actual smile seemed like spotting a yeti. Who was this and what had she done with Shaday?

"Scoot closer."

Elke scoffed. *"You* scoot."

"I'm too exhausted to move," Shaday whined.

Elke laughed, her blonde curls bouncing over her shoulders as she shifted beside the splayed-out princess. Shaday nestled her head on Elke's lap and the blonde girl lifted a hand to stroke black braids out of the princess's face. I cocked my head to the side. These two were certainly close. I remembered Bernhardt saying part of the reason he'd been invited to the wedding had been his daughter's friendship with Shaday. I frowned. Last night, Elke had seemed as though she was having nearly as bad a night as I was. Was she not happy for Shaday? Maybe her dad's embarrassing remarks had put her in a bad mood.

I shook my head at myself. I'd been startled when I fell through the rug and had been transfixed by the dancing, but now I was just spying. I really should go... or ask them for directions. Though there didn't seem to be a way through the screen to the room beyond. I turned to leave, but paused out of curiosity when Elke spoke again.

She passed one of the gloves back to Shaday. "See, I tried smaller holes, but more of them, to hold the enchanted oil. That, plus the spells, allows you to hold the fire for longer without getting burned. You wouldn't have lasted more than a minute without the gloves."

Shaday grinned up at Elke. "You're a genius, you brilliant inventor, you."

Elke blushed and lifted her chin. "I am, aren't I."

Shaday turned her head and huffed. "I just kept picturing pummeling Ario's face the whole time." She punched the air.

Elke's mouth quirked to the side. "I don't blame you. You'd take him down, too."

"I know I would." Shaday frowned. "I'm firstborn and I could defeat Ario or any of his tribe in a fight, which is all they seem to care about in a leader—who can punch the hardest." She rolled her eyes. "I should be queen." She spoke quieter. "I should be able to marry who I like."

Elke nodded and stroked Shaday's head. "Agreed."

"This city is crumbling. We need to rebuild, encourage innovation." Her hands fluttered as she talked, her head still in Elke's lap. "But my father's old and tired and he lets Ario and the other tribe leaders bully him into enforcing their backwards laws."

Elke nodded. "Stupid tribes."

Shaday sighed. "No. They just represent the people. If my father went against the tribes, we'd have no one to lead.

They'd all defect and form their own government." She set her jaw.

"Hey." Elke leaned down and brought her elf-like face down to hover above Shaday's. "Things are changing. Calloon's got some underground movements going, your people *want* change."

Shaday sniffed. "By the time they come above ground I'll be an old lady."

Elke crinkled her large, pointed nose that curved up at the end. "Aw. You'll be so cute with all your wrinkles."

Shaday folded her arms across her chest. "I'll look exactly like my mother."

A door at the top of some stairs behind them flew open and a plump older woman in a dark red headscarf burst in. She sighed loudly. "I should have known I'd find you here. A princess hiding in a storage closet?" She shook her head and clicked her tongue. "You need to leave before your mother catches you and has you skinned. Or worse, has me skinned."

Shaday skittered to a sitting position and she and Elke turned to face the woman.

"Sorry, Muma." Shaday's brows rose. "Is my mother looking for me?"

Elke stood, then helped Shaday to her feet.

"No." Muma's face softened and she smoothed her apron, her eyes downcast. "No, but I was. I—I'm afraid the police need to have a word with you."

"Oh no—Muma, what is it?" Shaday moved toward the stairs, her brows drawn together.

The servant shook her head. "Not you, my princess. I am afraid it's Elke they need to speak with."

Elke slid past Shaday and climbed several steps, standing just below the servant. "Why?"

Muma shook her head. "This would be better coming from someone else."

Elke tugged her blonde brows together. "No, please tell me." She blinked her big blue eyes and I had the very uncomfortable sensation that again, I was intruding and should leave. I backed up, reaching behind me for the rug, but not before Muma spoke again.

"It's your father, dear. He was found dead in his tent, just now. The police suspect murder. I am so sorry to tell you this." She wrung her apron between her hands.

Elke slumped and Shaday caught her against her chest. "Thank you, Muma. I'll stay with Elke for now." She took a deep breath. "We'll find the officers in a few moments."

The servant nodded. "They're waiting in the parlor." She turned, cast one last worried glance over her shoulder, and then shut the door behind her.

I pressed a hand to my mouth and my stomach twisted. How awful; poor Elke.

Quiet sobs broke the near silence and I hesitated, afraid my exit would make noise and add worry to her grief.

"I am so sorry, so sorry." Shaday spoke into Elke's hair.

The blonde girl lifted her red face and shook her head. "You know how I felt about him." She sniffed. "I'm—I'm more upset with myself than anything, I think."

Shaday frowned. "Why?"

"Because—because my first feeling was relief." She sobbed again. "I'm a horrible daughter."

"No. He was a difficult man and you are a wonderful everything." Shaday hugged Elke tighter as she buried her face in the princess's shoulder. I held my breath and edged out of the room, slipping out from behind the heavy rug.

5

BIG BROTHER

After I'd wandered the riad for another half an hour, I finally ran into a servant and asked for directions. With his help, I found my way out of the palace and out into the sunshine. The riad faced the main square of the city, with its market booths and shops, so once I'd found my way out of the palace, getting to the wares was relatively easy. I patted my pocket to make sure I still had Maple's list, then made my way across the bustling square.

I moved to a side street and strolled down a twisting corridor lined with tall wooden doors that were reinforced with black iron braces. A slatted roof cast alternating bars of sunlight and shade across the heads of my fellow shoppers, crammed in tight around me. We moved forward as a pack.

Merchants called out prices and beckoned me to view their wares, which ranged from woven hats to colorful scarves to dangling star-shaped lamps that glinted with multicolored jewels. Posters with peeling edges plastered every open wall space. One touted a reward for information

on the armor stolen from the Royal Artifacts Museum.
Someone had graffitied the image of a yellow lion over it.

I jumped as I shuffled past another—a wanted poster for
Horace, the words in another language, but the image
unmistakably his. Others had moving images of men
turning into bears with X's through them. I couldn't read the
words but I frowned. The message was clearly anti-shifter. I
was beginning to see what Shaday had meant by backward
laws.

I stopped in front of a food stand. Fruits and spices lay
piled in baskets atop the table in a way that reminded me of
the colorful tiles that seemed to decorate every floor, wall,
and ceiling in Calloon. I bought a bag of spiced pistachios. I
moved on and tried samples of flaky pastries with crunchy
nut fillings and slices of tart fruits. I purchased a silk bag
and piled it full of items from Maple's list—a jar of chickpea
flour, a bag of dates, walnuts, and saffron. I was sure Wool
already had all of these items, but it was just like Maple to
not want to impose and use up his supply. My enchanted
quill crossed items off until only a flask of argan oil
remained. I leaned against a wall smothered in posters and
let the mass of other shoppers pass by me. Women strode by
with their dark hair wrapped in colorful scarves, while their
children skipped beside them and tugged at their hands.
Two men working neighboring stands pulled stools up and
sat down together to share a drink of something from
frosted glasses. I swallowed, and my parched throat burned.
Maybe I'd try a glass of the famed mint tea if I spotted a little
cafe. I bit my lip, wondering where one might find argan oil,
and debated if I should ask for directions. I sighed. This
would be a lot more fun with Maple, or Iggy, or Hank.

As I missed my friends, I absentmindedly watched the
crowd passing by. I startled when I locked eyes with another

—a man who stood in the center of the corridor staring at me. The shoppers flowed around him like an island in a river. Chills crept up the back of my neck. I didn't recognize him, and yet something about his expression—the half-closed eyes, the confident smirk—seemed familiar. With his brimmed hat, button-up shirt, and leather messenger bag brimming with rolls of papers, he reminded me of Indiana Jones. Perhaps he was an archaeologist? But as I stared, his face changed, just for a flash and I saw my brother, Horace.

Mixed emotions raced through me and my breath quickened. Strangers passed between us and cut me off from him. I stepped back into the crowd, shouldering my way toward him. I'd been trying for months to think of a way to contact him and now he showed up here, in the Fire Kingdom? A man grumbled at me in another language as he slammed into my side, but I ignored him and rose up on my toes, trying to see over the scarved heads of the crowd. I couldn't lose him, not now. The crowd thinned and I reached the place where he'd stood, but he'd already gone. My heart sunk heavy in my chest and I looked left, then right, panicked. Where had he gone? Had I imagined it again, like at the feast last night? Or had he really been there?

The crowd parted for a just a few moments, long enough for me to spot my brother, wearing the stranger's face as a disguise again. He'd slipped down an arched alleyway, darker and quieter than the main thoroughfare. He gave a slight jerk of his head, motioning for me to follow, then turned and strode away. Adrenaline flooded through me and set my whole body tingling. Finally. I was finally going to meet my brother and get some answers. I pushed through the crowd and didn't care when I stumbled, or when a woman with three children shook her fist at me. I mumbled my apologies, but never took my eyes off Horace.

I reached the arched entryway to the winding alley, dotted with doors and crates and skittering mice. The temperature dropped as I entered, due to the solid roof that shaded the space. The echoes of my brother's footsteps on the paved ground mingled with mine, as I jogged forward, Horace always staying just barely visible around the next bend. Maple's concerns floated back to me. If he wanted to hurt me, he'd gotten me alone down a dark alley. No one knew where I was and I'd gone far enough from the market-place that I was out of sight, and probably out of hearing if I screamed... if anyone even heard me over the clamor of the crowd and the yelling merchants. Goose bumps prickled my arms despite the heat of the desert day. Feeling less confi-dent, I rounded a bend in time to catch sight of the heel of Horace's boot behind an open wooden door. It slammed shut behind him.

I stopped and considered my options. Option A, I could enter this back alley door to meet with my brother, who was known for being an international terrorist. Not sounding all that smart. Or option B, I could turn back and rejoin my friends in the safety of the riad. I sighed. Over the last few months, I'd tried talking with Hank and Maple about my curiosity about Horace. The more I thought about it, the more I felt there must be some kind of mistake. He couldn't be as bad as the rumors said he was if he'd been as kind and brave as Junie claimed he was as a child. Maybe he was some kind of Robin Hood, trying to expose a government cover-up to help out the little guy and had a bad rap because of negative propaganda. When I brought that up, Hank always came back to Horace trying to hurt me during the Summer Sea Carnival. I'd argued that he just wanted to talk, but Hank said, "You don't have to kidnap people to talk to them." I looked at the door and sighed. I knew what Hank and my friends would tell me to do. But if I listened to them and ran away, I'd never know what Horace wanted to tell me.

I bit my lip so hard it ached and looked left, toward the marketplace, then right toward the door Horace had disappeared through. I took a shaky breath, held it for the count of four, then let it out slowly, like Wool had taught Wiley and me. I nodded to myself, my mind made up. Red pill it was. I moved right, gripped the twisted iron handle of the unmarked door, and yanked it open. Time to see how deep the rabbit hole went.

6

CANTINA

I stepped into a dark space and blinked in an attempt to adjust my eyes. I stepped forward, my hands out in front of me. My stomach lurched as my foot passed through empty air and slid down several steps before I landed hard on my backside.

"Ow."

I had to stop doing that. As my eyes adjusted, I realized I'd slipped down a narrow staircase covered in black tiles. I pushed myself to my feet, my hip aching even worse now after my earlier fall through the hanging rug in the riad. I braced a hand against a wall to steady myself, but immediately pulled it away from the sticky surface and curled my lip in disgust. *Gross.* A warbly woman's voice singing with lackluster emotion floated up to me and I slowly descended the remaining few steps into a cantina. I was only about average height, by no means tall, and yet my head nearly reached the low ceiling braced with beams and exposed pipes. Without windows, the only light came from a few dusty lanterns that hung over the long bar and above a few tables, casting dim pools of light in the haze.

A man stood behind the bar and stacked dirty glasses. He looked up at me and narrowed his eyes. *Friendly place.* But, being sunken and dark, it was at least cooler than outside. I rubbed my bare arms and wished for a sweater... and not just for the cold. Disheveled men sat huddled around the tables and at the bar, hovering just outside the pools of light in clouds of hookah smoke, as though they had their own weather systems. Dark eyes flicked my way and stayed for too long. I gulped and stepped deeper into the cantina, scanning for Horace. I spotted the singer, a droopy woman propped in the corner with an entire bottle of wine clutched in her hands. She looked like part of the decor, like one of the many broken, dusty items piled onto the shelves behind the bar, or the graffiti scrawled across every inch of wall.

"Pretty girl for a place like this."

I jumped at the raspy voice and turned to find a tall, oily man leering over me.

I swallowed. "Horace?" My voice came out smaller than I liked.

He leaned closer, his breath reeking of alcohol and sweet tobacco. "That your boyfriend?"

I'd take that as a no. I stepped away and scanned the cantina, looking for Horace, but the man edged closer. He held out a bottle of beer. "Have a drink."

My eyes slid to the bottle, then up at the hairy man with the red-rimmed eyes. That drink was definitely spelled, not that I would have tried any of it anyway. "No thanks." I gulped. "I'm meeting someone."

I moved away from him, but he darted in front of me and blocked my path. "Don't be rude." His upper lip curled back and his hand slid to the large knife at his belt. *Great.*

My stomach turned with unease and with the cloying smell of sweet hookah smoke trapped in this windowless dungeon.

"Ahh!" The man screamed as the bottle in his hand shattered and foaming beer poured to the floor. I jumped back and stared at the puddle as the golden liquid turned pink. My breath quickened as I tried to understand what was happening. The man screamed again and clutched at his hand, which curled in a tight fist around the broken shards of the bottle, blood falling to the ground to mix with the spilled beer. A few patrons looked up and the bartender grumbled to himself, but no one moved to help.

"You were very rude to my sister."

My breath caught. I turned to my right and found Horace beside me, wearing his disguise. His eyes were hard as he stared at the cringing man. "Apologize."

The man hissed something at Horace in a language I didn't understand and then convulsed in pain as his hand tightened around the shards with a sickening crunch.

"What did you say?" Horace's voice came out low, but deadly.

The man panted and winced. "I—I'm sorry."

"Say it to her." Horace tipped his head at me.

The man whined, but turned to me. "I'm sorry." His hand flew open and I gasped. Shards of glass stayed embedded in his blood-smeared palm.

"Leave."

Trembling, the man scuttled past us without a moment's hesitation and flew up the steps. Light flooded the black stairs before fading as the door slammed shut.

Horace sighed and turned to me. "I'm afraid we've gotten off to a difficult start. I hope that didn't alarm you too much."

His deep-set eyes searched my face. "I expect you're quite afraid of me." He let his disguise drop and revealed his true face.

I let out a shaky breath. It was true, it had been a frightening display of power. And yet I felt grateful that Horace had intervened. Grateful, in fact, for all Horace had done for me, including saving me when I was a baby and he was just a little boy himself. I hated that he'd think me afraid of him.

I eased closer to him, gaging his reaction. I really didn't think he intended to hurt me... but I could be wrong. And yet, I'd gone my whole life thinking I was all alone and here I had my brother standing before me. I didn't know if I'd get this chance again. I took a deep breath, held it, and threw my arms around him.

"Thank you. Thank you for always protecting me."

He stiffened, but I held on tight and after a moment pulled back.

"Not a big hugger, huh?" I grinned and he stared at me with the same laconic expression as in his wanted posters. I searched his face for any resemblance to me and wondered if he looked more like our mother or our father? I didn't remember either one. He gave me a slow blink, his lids hanging low over his pale blue eyes. He looked bored. Maybe I was boring. A muscle jumped in his sharp jaw. I had full cheeks, so no similarity there. Even his upturned nose was different, as mine curved slightly down at the end. I sighed.

He lifted a brow, though the rest of his expression remained unmovable. "Not what you expected?"

My lips quirked to the side and I shook my head. "It's not that. I just—I wish I saw more of myself in you." I shrugged and pulled my lips into a half-hearted smile. "It's silly, I know. I just, well, I don't remember our parents and it'd be nice to see some resemblance." I forced a chuckle. "I wish I'd inherited those cheekbones."

His full lips quirked to the side and I beamed. I should not be so happy at making him almost smile... but I was.

He jerked his head behind him. "C'mon. I have a table for us. This is a conversation to be had in private."

I followed, happy to get out of sight of the other patrons, who'd watched the incident with the bottle all too closely. He gestured to a booth in an alcove by itself. I slid into the torn green leather seat. He followed, sitting across from me, and placed his bag of scrolls beside him. He'd really gone all out for that archaeologist disguise.

"It won't be long before someone recognizes me from the posters and alerts the authorities." He gave a lazy shrug. "There's quite a bounty on my head."

I gulped and looked around. "Shouldn't we go then?" I frowned. "Why did you drop the disguise?"

He blinked, slowly. "I wanted to see your reaction, see if I could trust you." He laced his hands together. "You panicked last time we spoke."

I cast back through my memory. Oh. He meant when he tried to pull me through a magic portal after revealing he'd been disguised as a circus strongman for a week without telling me. *A man he'd killed*, a little voice at the back of my head reminded me. I licked my lips. "You surprised me then. I didn't know—well, I didn't know what I do now. I thought you were trying to hurt me."

Horace laced his long, pale fingers together. They looked sickly under the dim light. "An understandable reaction." His eyes lifted to mine. "My apologies."

I waved my hand. "It's in the past. But uh, shouldn't you be going if you might be caught?"

His lips parted into a sly grin. "They won't catch me... not until I'm ready to be caught."

I frowned, not sure what to make of that.

"Besides." He leaned closer across the scratched table. "I'm trying a different approach with you. I thought we could ease into a relationship, try taking it slow. Just a short meeting at first. Maybe longer next time."

I nodded. "I've been thinking up ways to get in touch with you ever since you sent us to Wee Ferngroveshire."

"You're a survivor." A lock of brown, wavy hair fell across his eye. "You should call it Monsters Rise."

I nodded, my throat tight. A strange mix of excitement and terror coursed through me as I stared at the stranger who was my brother. "Right. Well, I wanted to thank you for saving me and—and I want to get to know you better. The truth of you." I held up my hand. "Not all the rumors."

He stared me down, unflinching.

"Unless... the rumors are true?" I gave a weak chuckle.

"Some are." Horace sniffed. "And it's about time you started seeing the truth of things."

Great. I seemed to be putting my foot in my mouth.

"What can I tell you?"

I let out the breath I'd been holding. Maybe he didn't hate me already. "Um... everything. Maybe it'd be good to start at the beginning, what happened at Wee—at Monsters Rise, when we were children?" I bounced my leg, my nerves getting the best of me.

Horace sighed. "A lifetime ago. What did the old woman, Junie, tell you?"

"That our mother was a mirror maker, and you were bright and loving and learning from her. That monsters came unannounced one night and destroyed the town... killed almost everyone. She said you ran, with me in your arms." Tears trickled down my cheeks and my chest lurched as I held in a sob. "She said you buried me in the snow and when she came to, you were gone, but she heard me crying and rescued me."

He looked away. The grimy overhead light cast sharp shadows from his cheek bones. "And then what?"

"And then... and then she survived as best she could, avoiding raiders and gangs until we made it to a human city. She adopted me out to the Bankses, they raised me in the US."

The muscle in his jaw twitched again. "That's why I couldn't find you. I looked for you, you know? You were with humans." He turned to face me. "She should have kept you with our people."

I shook my head. "She did the best she could, and the Bankses took good care of me." I slid my hand across the rough table and gave his wrist a squeeze. "Just like you did. I owe you, and her, my life."

He sniffed. "Don't forget the Swallow."

I froze. "The what?"

He cocked his head to the side. "You didn't hear that part, hm?"

I shook my head.

Horace's eyes flitted to his folded hands, mine still resting on his wrist, then up to my face. "The monster that chased us up the hill was hideous. It had rows of sharp teeth and grabbing hands that plucked men up and ate them whole."

My chin trembled.

"Luckily, our parents avoided being eaten. Instead they were crushed when the first few monsters burst from the mirror shop below our rooms and the house collapsed."

My eyes welled with tears. "The monsters... came

through the mirrors?" I gulped, my throat tight. "Junie suspected something like that."

He nodded. "Yes. A piece of the puzzle it took me many years to understand."

"How did we escape if our parents were killed?"

He shrugged. "The noise was horrendous. We woke immediately. They had time to shove you into my arms and toss us out the window. The snow was deep and I landed in a drift. Our home collapsed before they could follow."

I pressed a hand to my mouth as a tear rolled down my cheek.

"There wasn't time to cry or search the rubble. More monsters exploded from the wreckage and slithered and scrambled after us. I ran, with you in my arms, as the old woman told you. Screams, horrible screams, followed me. My legs ached and my chest burned as I trudged through the deep snow, you just a baby in my arms. I ran for our lives."

I shook my head. How horrible.

"The thing with the rows of teeth had a tail that whipped, side to side, and it caught me in the back and sent me flying into the snow, you buried beneath me. I just lay there, unable to move my legs. It had broken my back."

I uttered a little cry and squeezed his wrist.

"I feared I'd smother you. I managed to shove you out from under me. At least my arms still worked. Some snow must have covered me, or maybe the monster moved on to bigger meals, but it left us to freeze to death. I lay there, shivering until I couldn't feel anything anymore, listening to the screams and roars grow quieter and more infrequent, until I heard nothing at all." His lips quirked to the side. "Everyone was dead. Even you stopped crying."

I let out a shuddering gasp.

Horace cleared his throat. "The next thing I felt was warmth. It spread from my heart outward. It was golden and safe and electric. I could breathe again, could feel my fingers again—and then, blissfully, my legs. I thought for a moment it had all been a horrible dream. I rolled over to my back and found myself staring straight up into the face of a new monster. I opened my mouth and screamed. It dipped its face to mine and turned its head this way and that, like a curious bird. It had large, round eyes and I could see my reflection in them. A puny child, about to be eaten. But then it closed those eyes and the giant thing bent lower and placed its forehead against the whole of my body and the warmth deepened until I felt tingly and whole and light. It was the Swallow. It told me its name, somehow, without words. It said that it could give magic force to heal, but that it would change me. And I no longer felt afraid." Horace cocked his head to the side and looked at me across the table. "You see, Imogen? Not all monsters are evil." His lips quirked into a sardonic smile.

I sniffled and squeezed his wrist tighter. My brows pulled together. "I don't think you're evil."

His eyes widened, ever so slightly. He turned his head and cleared his throat.

"She healed you, too. You were frostbitten and nearly dead."

I shook my head, trying to process all of this. "So that's why we're swallows? Because of the creature that healed us? Huh." I bit my lip and thought of Hank. "Is that how all swallows get their powers?"

Horace gave me a lazy blink. I wasn't sure what to make of that.

He sighed. "The Swallow was the original. She pulled magical energy from outside herself and funneled it through her, to us, to heal. We've kept some of that power, I believe, and share the ability to pull magic from outside ourselves."

I blinked. "This is incredible." I thought about my abilities (or lack thereof) with magic. "You know, I have been able to send energy to Iggy before, he's my baking flame, to help him grow bigger. Is it the same kind of thing?"

"Perhaps." Horace chuckled, a deep sound. "You are capable of so much more than you know."

That could be ominous. I chose to take it as a friendly compliment and smiled. "I hope you'll teach me."

He nodded. "In time, I hope so as well."

"So, then what happened? Why weren't you beside me when Junie came to?"

"Ah. That." Horace licked his lips. "The old woman had reason to fear raiders and gangs. A group of such men came upon us. I had enough time to hide you, but they'd already spotted me. The Swallow was a gentle thing and fled to the forest. They took me and forced me to be a soldier in their child army until I grew up and became a soldier in their army of men."

I gaped. "You grew up enslaved?"

He winked. "They considered it more like indentured mercenary, but sure. It wasn't without its benefits. I learned to be cunning and fierce."

"How did you escape?" I felt like the biggest jerk in the world for ever feeling upset with my adopted family.

"We did a job for a nobleman, in title only, protecting his keep from some rival gang that was out for blood for some deal gone awry. He was an arms dealer, mostly, but dealt in anything that would make him money. And this was the time right after the treaty when the wilderness still stretched across most of the kingdoms. Well, this noble had never met a Swallow before, we are rarer than you know, Imogen, and he was impressed with my abilities."

I frowned. "What abilities?"

"There are many things we can do because of our access to an unlimited supply of magic. There are spells no one has ever thought of because they could not imagine having enough power to pull them off." His lips quirked to the side. "I have a lot to show you."

A cool wave washed over my stomach, unease at the vagueness of his answer.

"So this man bought me from my captors and I worked several years for him. He dealt with many rich and powerful people, royalty even, and I learned their secrets, as well as his. I learned some truths that needed righting and so I got out of the mercenary business and set myself to the revenge business."

I gulped. "The Badlands Army?"

He nodded. "Precisely."

I blinked down at the table, trying to process everything he'd told me. I looked up. "You met Hank once, right? You both remembered each other, last summer at the carnival."

Horace blinked. "I'd met your golden prince before the carnival, yes."

I sighed, so enigmatic. "Can't you tell me more? I want to know everything about you."

Horace held up a finger and looked back over his shoulder. "Do you hear that?" he whispered.

I held still. "I don't hear anything."

"It's too quiet. No singing, no murmur of voices. The police have arrived, I imagine."

My heart raced.

"We met at this rat hole because criminals will hesitate to rat out another—they risk being caught themselves. But I imagine the price on my head is high enough to risk it." He shrugged. "It's time to leave." His mask of the other face slid into place, my brother gone. Horace shouldered his bag of papers and stood, gesturing for me to do the same. I grabbed the bag of spices and foods I'd purchased in the market and slid out of the booth as quietly as I could. He pointed behind me. "There's a back door there."

I moved to the back of the alcove. The black door blended into the black wall, and in the dim light I'd have never seen it if Horace hadn't pointed it out. I slipped out and just as the door closed behind us, shouts came from the cantina.

"He was just there, with a girl!"

"They went out the back."

I gasped and Horace pointed down the alleyway. "That'll lead you back to the main square. Run, I'll lead them off."

I dashed away a few steps then spun around. "How will I contact you again?"

Horace whirled. "I'll find you. I always will."

Warmth flood my chest for a moment and I nodded— that was sweet. I frowned... or was it a threat?

Horace turned and ran, and I did the same, heading in the opposite direction. My heart thundered in my chest and I didn't stop until I'd reached the safety of the crowds in the main square before the palace. I slumped against a wall and wiped the sweat from my brow and upper lip. As my chest heaved, I struggled to make sense of everything that had just happened. A monster, a Swallow, had healed Horace and me as children, giving us our unique powers. Horace wanted a relationship with me and though he was powerful and dangerous and had lived a hard life, he hadn't tried to hurt or coerce me. I blew out a heavy breath.

One thing was certain though. I now had some enormous secrets, and wasn't sure I could tell any of my friends or Hank about them.

7

TENT TALKS

E motionally and physically exhausted (I needed to do more cardio) I dragged myself back to the riad. I'd barely been let in to the central courtyard by one of the palace servants before Amelia rounded the corner and pounced on me.

"There you are."

"Here I am." I yawned.

Her jaw dropped as she looked me over and shook her head. "You look a mess."

"Gee, thanks Amelia." I stepped forward, planning on heading to the kitchen, but she stepped in my way.

"Where do you think you're going?" She crinkled her nose. "Ugh, you smell like stale smoke and beer. Where have you been?"

I held up the heavy bag of spices and fruits. The glass jars clinked together. "I went to the market to pick some things up for Maple, so I'm just going to head to the kitchen and drop them off."

"Oh no you're not."

I lifted a brow in surprise. "I'm not?"

Amelia held out a slender arm and made a grabby hand gesture. "Hand it over."

I lifted the bag and raised my brows in question, and she nodded. I passed it to her and she immediately gave it to the servant who'd let me in. "Please deliver this to the bakery at your earliest convenience." The servant bowed and moved past us through the courtyard where birds chirped and the calming sound of trickling water issued from the fountain.

I folded my arms. "You're seriously not letting me in? Where am I supposed to go?"

Amelia stepped closer and squeezed my upper arms. Her face softened. "I'm sorry. It's just, this is the biggest event of my career—planning a royal wedding? Come on, it's all I've ever dreamed of, and I'm a *bit* stressed. You know I love you, right?"

I nodded.

"Good." Her face hardened. "Because that was friend Amelia talking. Now this is event planner Amelia."

I frowned. "Can't I just keep talking to friend Amelia?"

She shook her head. "No. She's gone and event planner Amelia will not let you ruin the biggest day of her life."

I scoffed. "Don't you mean the biggest day of Hank's and Shaday's lives?"

"No. They don't care as much as I do. Trust me. I heard what happened earlier and I cannot have your mess of emotions destroying everything I've worked for."

My jaw dropped. "It wasn't that bad. It was just a batch of macaroons."

"Imagine if it had been the wedding cake and hundreds of elite guests had tasted your angst and bitterness?"

"Uh!" I curled my lip in indignation.

"Friend Amelia here, and I totally understand how hard

it must be for you to watch Hank get married. So maybe it's best if you took a break from this one?"

"Wait, is that what friend or event planner Amelia thinks?" My brain was starting to hurt.

"Friend Amelia is phrasing it as a suggestion, while business me is making it an order. Stay away from the bakery until you can keep your emotions under control. Which, let's be real, is only going to get less likely the closer we get to the big day. So let's just say, stay out of the bakery until we get back to Bijou Mer."

I frowned and my voice rose to a whine. "Amelia, what am I supposed to do then? Just twiddle my thumbs? Come on, I'm a baker. It's what I do."

She turned me around and marched me back out of the palace. "Not today it isn't."

A few servants waited, mounted on camels, while a couple more held the reins of two riderless camels.

Amelia swept her hand toward them. "Today you're going back out to the base of Damavash to clean up the site from last night's feast."

I rolled my eyes. "Oh goodie."

"Come on, I'm going with you. It'll be—well, it'll be a good distraction. And hey!" She flashed a bright smile that matched her tightly coifed white hair. "The smell of the camels will cover up your odor."

I flashed a sarcastic smile back. "Oh boy!"

She rolled her eyes and with the help of the handlers, we mounted the camels and took off for the camp.

THE QUIET OF the camp during the day contrasted sharply with the music, lights, laughter, and general hubbub of the night before. Some of the lull may have had something to do with the police presence. A few Fire Kingdom officers in red stood to the side of the tents and spoke in low voices with Urs Volker and a few other Air Kingdom officers wearing black. I turned my head, trying to listen in.

Clank!

I jumped and brought my attention back to the task at hand. Amelia had taught me a new spell, well, a variation on one I knew. She'd put me to work not only levitating dirty plates, glasses, and utensils, but also had me directing the floating parade of cutlery into various chests and cases to be transported back to the riad and washed there. Only I'd gotten distracted and now my parade was experiencing a traffic jam. I took a deep breath and concentrated. I willed the never-ending line of dishes to their places, and the pace picked up again. Amelia had gone off to coordinate some-thing or other, while the other palace servants watered the camels at the oasis and broke down the tables and chairs.

After a full hour of mind-numbing plate levitation, while standing in the sun no less, I decided I deserved a break. I hadn't seen Amelia in ages to let her know, so I figured I'd just pop over to the oasis and soak my feet for a minute, and be back before she noticed. I pulled my hair out of its band as I walked between tents, their canvas snapping in the breeze. I pulled a strand of the red hair to my nose and sniffed. I made a face. Amelia had not been lying—I stank. I followed the sound of camel grunts and swishing palm fronds toward the pool of water. But as I rounded a corner, I paused.

Up ahead stood Bernhardt Beckham's tent, where I'd seen him arguing with that journalist, Ms. L'Orange, the night before. I frowned as I remembered the heated conver-sation. She'd wanted something Bernhardt had. Maybe whatever it was, was in his tent. Maybe she'd wanted it bad enough to kill him for it. I walked closer and looked right, then left. The officers stood a good distance away, absorbed in their conversation with each other. I wasn't officially a detective, but I'd had a part in solving a few murders recently, and if I was banned from the kitchen maybe I could at least be helpful in pinning down Bernhardt Beckham's murderer. The tent flaps blew open as I approached, as if beckoning me to come in and investigate. There was no police tape, no guards standing outside. I bit my lip. Maybe I should just go to the police and tell them about the argument I'd overheard. But I didn't want to get Ms. L'Orange in trouble for no reason, and I hadn't had the best experiences with police officers in the past. I peeked into the tent. Maybe I'd find something inside that would give me a clearer sign as to whether she might be guilty or not. With one last glance toward the officers standing about, I ducked inside.

"Oh."

I stopped short, not sure where to stand. A metal trunk stood open at the foot of the black wrought iron bed, with papers and clothes pouring out of it and even more items littered all over the floor. The sheets and thin white blanket had been tossed aside, and the mattress hung halfway off the bedframe. Two leather armchairs sat in the corner of the peaked white tent, with a small round table between them. Two wineglasses lay overturned on the table, a purplish red stain beside the bottle. I tiptoed over the bunched-up oriental rug and around a stack of crumpled papers and examined the stain. It appeared to be wine, not blood. I let out the breath I'd been holding.

In fact, there didn't seem to be any obvious signs of blood around. I was about to move away when I gave the glasses a second look. There were two glasses, each with a little stain of red wine in the bottom. That meant someone had been here with him last night, someone he knew well enough to entertain. I remembered the smarmy way he'd looked at Ms. L'Orange and called her Maddie. Maybe it was someone he wanted to know better. I moved closer to the bed. A cracked mirror sat atop a side table, and to the right of that was a simple wooden desk and chair. The chair lay on its side and the contents of the drawers had been dumped out on the floor.

I let out a sigh. Someone had been looking for something. Madeline was seeming guiltier in my book by the minute. I heard voices approaching and froze. Shadows passed across the fabric of the tent and I had only a moment to dive behind the overturned desk before the tent flaps opened and two men stepped inside. I held my breath and pressed a hand to my racing chest. I was so dumb. Interfering in a crime scene in another country—not good. And that was if they didn't just outright charge me with the murder. I mean, I looked pretty guilty skulking around. I winced and prayed they'd leave quickly, without finding me.

"...as zuch, za need for diplomacy is high. Vee are in a foreign kingdom and cannot do as vee vould normally."

I groaned inwardly as I recognized the voice—Urs Volker, Bernhardt's head of security.

"Da, Varden Volker."

I raised my brows and stared at some strewn papers and open books lying on the ground next to my head. Warden, huh? I guess with Bernhardt's death, Urs became the head of the prison. So Urs had a motive.

"But make no mishtake. I fully plan to find za killer and see zem punished—to za full extent of za law."

Urs and the other officer continued their conversation in what I guessed to be German, and the shoulder I lay on began to ache. If they were going to find me, could they just hurry up and do it? I cocked my head to the side as I spotted something odd. I reached up slowly, careful to make no sound, and tugged on the silky bit of flowery fabric. It tore slightly, and I realized it was caught on a nail on the underside of the desk. I worked it loose and brought it close to my face to look it over.

It looked like part of a scarf, and the flower pattern with the bright yellow and fuchsia colors made me guess it belonged to a woman. Madeline had been wearing a scarf last night, but from a distance in the dark, I hadn't been able to make out the pattern of the fabric. I rolled my eyes. Then again, just about every woman here wore a head scarf or loose gauzy dresses. That didn't help much. I rubbed the soft, loosely woven fabric between my fingers. I should probably hand this over to the police. And yet, my experience with our own head of police, Inspector Bon, hadn't inspired me with confidence in them. And now that it appeared Urs might have had a motive to kill his boss, I didn't feel particularly trusting toward him, either. I slowly slid the scrap of fabric into the pocket of my jeans.

Urs slipped back into English. "I personally placed massive security shpells on Beckham's tent. Anyone who attempted to enter visout permission vould have become violently ill."

The other officer spoke. "So you sink Beckham let za killer in heemself?"

Urs didn't answer but paper crinkled under feet as the men moved toward the armchairs in the corner. I bit my lip and hoped they couldn't see me from that angle.

"He brought za blueprints for za renovations to Carclaustra een hees trunk. He hoped to get zome vork done zis veek."

"Vee haf found no blueprints, Varden Volker."

"I know. Zey ave been shtolen. I ave already sent vord back to za prison to double up on security. Someone now has knowledge of za layout. Eet ees not enough to breach security, but who knows vat ees planned. Vee must shtay vigilant."

"Da, Varden Volker."

I frowned. Stolen blueprints? What would Madeline want with blueprints? And if Urs killed Bernhardt and stole the blueprints himself, who was he trying to frame?

"Vee are shtill vaitink for za official report, but I saw za body. No blood—except on za medal at hees throat."

"So... eet vas the murderer's?"

Urs spoke again. "Eet seems so. But vee must vait for za official vord. Vee must shtick to protocol, and not allow our own feelinks of grief cloud our judgement."

He didn't sound that upset to me.

"*Da*, Varden Volker."

"Come, let us return to za city and see if za coroner has news. Vee have done all vee can here."

Yes, I willed them. *Yes, leave for the city*.

Papers crinkled underfoot as the men retraced their steps. Warm sunlight flooded the tent as the flaps opened. The room darkened as the opening fell shut behind the officers.

Urs's voice came more muffled now, from outside. "I am goink to reseal za tent, to preserve za crime scene."

My heart stopped. Oh no. I'd be trapped inside.

"Inform za local officers zat eef zey need entrance, to zimply contact me."

"*Da*, Varden Volker."

I rolled to my hands and knees and scrambled as quickly and quietly as I could around the desk, past the trunk and to the opposite side of the bed. Urs's shadow lifted its arms, a wand in one hand.

Oh no, oh no, oh no.

I tugged up the side of the tent and dragged myself out, lying flat on my stomach. My toe had just cleared the canvas when a shimmery force field glossed over the whole of the tent. I let out a shaky sigh. That had been a close one. I plunked my forehead down on my folded arms.

A shadow fell over me and I slowly lifted my head, my mind racing for excuses to tell the officers about why I was lying beside a murdered man's tent.

"There you are."

I blinked up at Amelia. My eyes struggled to focus against the bright sun behind her.

She let out a heavy sigh. "Lying down on the job. Come on, we have loads more to clean up."

She grabbed my arm and helped me to my feet. I dusted sand off my legs and arms, while Amelia looked me over with disapproval. I supposed that being covered in dirt wasn't helping my appearance.

"You're going in the back entrance when we get back to the riad."

"Amelia!" I planted my hands on my hips. "I'm not having the best day, okay?"

"I would hug you, but...." Amelia gestured from my dirty shirt to the white backless jumpsuit she wore. I could only dream of pulling that outfit off half as well as she did.

I tipped my head to the side. "Fair enough."

"But friend Amelia thinks you deserve a lemonade and some leftover treats from last night." She grabbed my hand.

I grinned. "Lead the way."

As we moved off, I noticed a long black hair stuck to my hand. My first instinct was to shake it off, but then I realized it must have stuck to me when I was crawling through Bernhardt's tent. All of the officers I'd seen, both from the Air and Fire Kingdoms, had short cropped hair in the military style, as had Bernhardt. Amelia wore her curly white hair barely half an inch long, and my own was red. Perhaps it belonged to the killer.

8

MAID SERVICE

True to her word, after we'd finished cleaning up the party site and had returned to the city, Amelia made me enter through the back of the palace, off the alley. Covered in sand and reeking of stale hookah smoke and sweat from the heat of the day, I felt like something the cat dragged in.

Amelia gave me directions back to the room I was sharing with Maple, K'ree, and Annie on the second floor of the palace, but of course, I got lost again. The place was like a maze of hallways, arched doors, potted plants, and small gardens and atriums. One beautifully tiled room blended into the next, and the next. I considered just lying down in the middle of the hallway and taking a nap.

I was feeling pretty bad for myself when I dragged my feet around a corner, my eyes on the ground, and slammed into someone.

"Oof!"

I gasped and held out my hands. "I'm so sorry, are you okay, I wasn't—" I blinked at the young woman in front of me. She was dressed in the red and gold veils of the palace staff and carried a tall stack of white towels embroidered with gold thread. She peeked around the stack and curtsied.

"My apologies, miss."

It took me a moment to place her, but I recognized her as the server who'd purposely spilled on Bernhardt last night. She stepped to the side to move past me, but I side-stepped and blocked her.

"Hey, I recognize you from the feast last night." My legs ached and my dry tongue scraped the roof of my mouth. I needed rest and water and my mind wasn't firing on all cylinders, but I scrambled to come up with a line of questioning. She clearly disliked Bernhardt—she counted as a suspect. Plus, she had long black hair, so the one in the tent could've been hers.

She blinked her dark eyes. "I was working, yes." She looked me up and down. "Do... you need a towel?" She lifted her brows, clearly wondering why I was holding her up.

I waved a hand and tried to act cool. "No. I mean, yes, I will for a shower. I mean, look at me, right? If anyone needs to clean up, it's this girl." I jabbed my thumbs at myself and chuckled. She just stared. I cleared my throat. "But not one of those, I have towels up in my room. I just wanted to ask you—uh—did you hear about Bernhardt? Bernie, his friends called him... maybe."

She frowned. "Were you his friend?"

"No." I shook my head. Why had I said that? Must be heatstroke. I lifted my brows. "Were you?"

"No."

This was going well. "He uh, he seemed like a real jerk though, huh?"

She blinked at me and shifted the large, and surely heavy, stack of towels. Her loose sleeve slid up her arm, revealing a crescent moon tattoo on the inside of her wrist. Huh. I'd only ever seen tattoos on the backs of hands and lower arms. She caught me staring and shrugged the sleeve back over it.

"Hey, uh, I could help you with those, that looks heavy." I reached my grimy arms out and she jerked back, turning away to shield the pure white towels. I didn't blame her.

"No, miss. You are a guest."

And my grimy arms undoubtedly also factored into that decision. I tipped my head side to side. "Well, I work in the palace back in Bijou Mer, so you know, us working girls have to stick together. And from what I hear, Bernhardt had it coming." I nodded, waiting for some sign of her agreement. It never came. I licked my lips. She stepped forward and out of desperation I blurted out, "I mean, I would have killed him if I'd had the chance, so if you know who did, or even if you did him in yourself, I wouldn't tell anyone." I wanted to slap myself.

She frowned, her eyes wide, and gave me a wide berth as she moved past. "I wouldn't know about that, miss. Good day."

I sighed. Yeah, I'd say good day to me too, if I were her. I'd barely taken a step forward around the corner before I spotted Hank at the far end of the long hallway coming toward me, Francis hovering just behind. I leapt out of sight and scrambled backward. I slammed, once again, into the poor servant.

"Ahh!" She screamed, understandably, and whirled around.

I winced and held a finger to my lips. "I am so sorry. But if you could just keep your voice down, I'd really appreciate that."

Her eyes grew wider until I could see the whites all

around her pupils. "Why?" She barely breathed the word. "Are you going to kill me?" She took a deep breath, presumably to scream, but I shook my head.

"No. No. I just saw someone I'm avoiding like the plague right now." Because my last encounter with Hank had been awkward (my fault), because I'd just met with my fugitive brother and Hank was a prince and sworn to uphold the law, and also because I looked like a piece of human trash.

She backed away, looking me up and down. "You have the plague? Many of the other servants are ill and I cannot afford to get sick myself." She edged away. "Rojer is the worst off... have you been spending time with him?"

I frowned. "Rojer?"

She nodded. "Ario Tuk's servant. He was sent to the infirmary. I've never seen anyone so ill." She curled her lip and eyed me with distrust.

I sighed. "I said *avoiding* like the plague, I don't *have* it."

She crinkled her nose and muttered. "You smell like you do."

Touchè.

Since the questioning had gone so well, I decided I had nothing further to say and bolted down the hallway, leaving the bewildered servant in my dust. A few twists and turns later I felt confident that I'd lost Hank... but I'd also gotten lost myself. Well, more lost. I sighed. I just wanted a shower... and some macaroons. Maybe Maple would sneak me some since I was banned from the bakery.

As I shuffled along, I became aware of another set of footsteps and paused. *Clip clip clip.* Shoot. Maybe I hadn't lost Hank. I slid into an alcove and peered around the corner. A slight woman, with long, straight black hair swung around the corner and headed down the tiled hallway towards me. I sighed with relief. It was Madeline L'Orange, the journalist who'd been arguing with Bernhardt... and my number-one suspect. Was it a bad sign that I felt relieved to be alone with a possible killer, instead of my boyfriend?

I cleared my throat and stepped out of the alcove, hoping this line of questioning would go better than the one I'd just attempted. She smiled slightly at me as she approached. I noted the old-fashioned camera hanging from a leather strap around her neck and the quill and scroll magically hovering beside her head as she walked.

"Hi, are you a reporter?"

The thin woman came to a stop in front of me. "A journalist, yes." She narrowed her almond-shaped eyes and her lips quirked to the side.

"Oh, cool. I, uh—" I racked my brain. "I was wondering—"

She pulled a card from her shirt pocket. The quill floated down and scribbled on it, then she handed it to me. "I'm working, covering the tea between the royal families, so I can't talk now, but I'd love to chat later. I'll be back tomorrow, but I'm staying on the second floor of the blue house across the main square from the palace. Ask around, everyone knows it."

I looked at her card. Below her typed name and profession, the quill had scribbled "blue house, second floor, door to the right of the landing" in blue ink.

"You look like a woman who spends time in alcoves and back alleys."

"Gee, thanks," I grumbled.

She laughed. "I just mean, you probably overhear things around the palace." She winked. "I pay very well for gossip. Never underestimate gossip." She tapped her card again before breezing past. "Look me up when you get off your shift. Anything you say is off record, of course."

Huh. I stared at her card as her footsteps faded. I had a lead.

9

THE NAKED TRUTH

After I showered and felt like a human woman again, I put on a fresh pair of jean shorts, a sleeveless button-up blouse, and a brimmed hat. My cheeks stung so I figured I'd gotten enough sun for the day. With Madeline's card in hand, I left the palace (after a few wrong turns) and made my way across the bustling main square. I asked a merchant for directions to the blue house and she pointed it out to me. Sure enough, nestled among the sand-colored buildings stood a square one painted bright blue. A cat darted into the narrow alley at the side of the house as I approached the front door.

The gated door opened with a squeak and clanked shut behind me. I found myself in a dingy foyer with numbered mailboxes on the left-hand wall and a pile of garbage bags to the right. I frowned, no longer so sure this was a great idea. I stepped past the trash and climbed the scuffed stairs. I stopped at the landing. Three doors opened off it, and per the card's direction, I rapped on the right-hand one. As I stood waiting for an answer, muffled shouts came from behind the other doors and overhead, footsteps thudded across the ceiling.

The door opened a crack. "What do you want?"

I cleared my throat. "I'm uh, the lurker you met earlier in the riad?"

The door flew open and Madeline beamed at me. "Well, look at you. I didn't recognize you clean." She waved me in and I followed behind her. She moved across the large, open room and stood behind a massive metal desk. I closed the door behind me and stood awkwardly by the door, unsure where to go. She shuffled some papers around, stacking some, tossing others toward the wastebasket, which she missed. If she was organizing, it was a system only Madeline could understand. Papers lay scattered everywhere around the studio. They sat in piles on the messy bed, littered the entire top of the desk, and were spread out all around the base of it as well. Some were full-sized sheets, but many looked like notes jotted down on receipts, napkins, and other scraps.

"Come in," she called, without looking up. "Please excuse the dump. My paper put me up here. You can tell I'm popular with my editor."

As if on cue, something rolled across the ceiling, followed by a startlingly loud thump, and then muffled shouts. I moved toward the desk, stepping over a pile of clothes, and then took a leap over a river of papers. To the right of the desk, a tall wardrobe stood bursting with clothes, scarves, and hats, while behind Madeline, dust particles floated in the dirty beams of light cast by the wall of slatted shutters. An old-fashioned ceiling fan turned slowly overhead.

Madeline pulled a quill from behind her ear and jotted a note down, then scribbled out a line of text, and passed the sheet to her right, where an enchanted quill scribbled furiously on another sheet of paper.

"I'm on deadline to get out not one, but two pieces. My paper still wants nonstop coverage of the nuptials of course, gossip sells, but Bernhardt's death is a big deal and I'm at ground zero. I've got three other papers interested in buying a piece on it. I've got to get it written before their own reporters arrive by airship to cover it."

I fiddled with an oil lamp that sat atop her desk. "I don't know much about him. Why is his death such a big deal?"

"Hmph." She scribbled out a whole paragraph and wrote some new words in the margins of the paper. "Well, he mingles with royalty and those in power—he had quite a bit himself. He trained fighters here in the Fire Kingdom, well Urs did really, about ten years ago, brought his daughter Elke with him. She and Princess Shaday became *quite* good friends." Madeline arched a brow, but never looked up from her desk. "So for a friend of the royalty, whose daughter is also connected to the princess, to be murdered on foreign soil? Raises a lot of questions."

It certainly did. Not only did Madeline have something she wanted back from Bernhardt, but murdering him would have given her the extra advantage of getting the scoop.

"I think I saw you two talking last night at the feast...did you know him personally?"

Madeline's dark eyes flicked to my face for a moment, then back down to her work. She sighed. "I do work that gets me paid, but my true passion is writing exposés. For years I've done work on human rights abuses, and it's no secret that Carclaustra under Bernhardt's management was one big human rights issue."

I tried to keep my tone neutral. "Sounds like a terrible guy. Guess you really hated him, huh?"

Madeline straightened up and planted a hand on her hip. She lifted a thin black brow. "I didn't kill him, if that's what you're getting at."

I raised my brows in surprise. Guess I hadn't been as subtle as I thought.

"The prisoners there have no rights, no ability to complain if they're treated badly, which they are. Rumor has it they're kept in solitary for twenty-three hours a day. That's torture, as far as I, and many laws, are concerned." She thumped the desk.

"Rumor? You don't know?"

She shook her head. "No one knows what it's like in there. You can't get in to tour it, and I've tried every angle to wheedle information out of the guards." She shook her head again. "Bernhardt has them taking his secrets to the grave. I've never seen a group of people so tight-lipped in my life. So no, Bernhardt was not my favorite person, but we've met several times over the years, in a professional capacity."

It had seemed like more than that to me last night. I glanced down, thinking it over, and caught something hiding under a pile of papers in the wastebasket beside the desk. I stepped to the side and bent over. Using two fingers, I pulled the yellow-and-pink flowered scarf through one of the openings in the wire and held it up. Madeline's face darkened. Sure enough, a corner of the scarf was ripped and missing.

"I found a piece of this scarf at the crime scene." My heart thundered in my chest. *I may be alone in a room with a killer.* At least I knew the walls were thin enough that someone would hear me scream if she attacked. "And I saw you arguing in front of his tent. You wanted something back from him. Did you want it bad enough to kill him for it?"

She stared at me, her nostrils flared and her eyes dark

for what seemed like eternity. She blinked and straightened up. "I don't have to speak to you."

"Fine, then I'll take this to the police and you can speak to them." Which was probably what I should have done in the first place. I edged backward toward the door.

Madeline rolled her eyes. "I didn't kill him, all right? You can take that to the police, but in the end, that's what they're going to find anyway." She stepped left, and moved around to the side of the desk.

I backed up. "What did you want from him? Why were you in his tent, if you didn't kill him?"

She folded her arms. "Why don't we make this worth both our whiles? I'll tell you what you want to know, but I want some palace gossip. I've got an article to write, after all."

"Fine." I gulped. "You start." I had no intention of giving her any gossip, but I'd have to come up with something.

She lifted her chin. "You saw us arguing because he was blackmailing me to keep me from publishing the article I'm writing about Carclaustra's abuses."

"With what?"

She took a deep breath and leaned her hip against the desk, then blew it out. "We had a tryst, over twenty years ago. I was young and foolish and believed his lies. He took photos of us together in bed, without my knowledge by the way. He was threatening to make them public. I'm respected for working on human rights issues. If it came out that I'd slept with the biggest human rights abuser there is, my professional reputation would be ruined."

I frowned. "That's terrible. But it'd give you a huge motive for killing him. Why did I find a piece of your scarf in his tent?"

She shook her head. "Your turn. What can you tell me? Something juicy, please."

I bit my lip and racked my brain. "Um... I overheard some maids saying there might be a mouse problem in the riad."

Madeline lowered her brows. "Really? I want secrets, not pest control issues."

I threw up my hands, the scarf still clenched in one. "I don't have anything else."

She shook her head. "Then you don't get any more information."

I backed up. "Fine. I'll take what I know to the police then."

She smirked. "Go for it. I'll burn the pictures before you get back and then it's your word against mine that that scarf belongs to me." She cocked her head to the side. "And how exactly did you find that scrap of fabric at the crime scene, by the way? Since you're not police, they may have some questions about why you were in the tent."

I gulped. She was right. I sighed. "Fine." My stomach turned with guilt at revealing another's secret, but if it would help solve a murder.... "Shaday has a secret lover."

Madeline stared at me for a beat, then chuckled and waved a hand. "Old news." She stood up and moved behind her desk and shuffled some papers.

I let out a heavy sigh. I hadn't wanted to tell Shaday's secret, and now it seemed I'd done it in vain. I didn't feel too good about myself.

Madeline sniffed, her eyes on her desk. She flipped a paper over. "Now, if you'd told me it was Prince Harry who had a mistress...."

I sucked in a quick breath of air and froze. She looked up and narrowed her eyes. Shoot! She'd noticed my reaction. A slow smirk spread across her face. "You know something."

I gulped and pressed my lips tight together, as if that would keep her from dragging any information out of me.

"Ho ho." Madeline grinned widely and straightened up. "Well now, that is news." She planted a hand on her hip, her elbow cocked wide. "Mr. Goody Two-shoes, Bijou Mer's sweetheart, has a fling on the side." Her gaze snapped to mine. "I want all the information you have. I'll pay you for it, a lot."

I lifted my chin, trying to act more confident than I was. She'd already guessed, and though there was no way I would tell her anything more, I figured I'd at least try to get something for it. "Not yet. Your turn. I want to know why I found your scarf in the tent."

Madeline considered a moment, then sat in the chair behind the desk and propped her feet up. "I went back to Bernhardt's later last night. I planned to flirt my way into the tent, lead him on long enough to dig about and find the photos, and then bolt." She shrugged and her face fell. "But when I got there, the lamps were on inside, but I got no answer. I went in and found him dead, sprawled on the floor, the whole place looked like it'd been ransacked." She shook her head. "Bit of a shock, that one."

"You didn't call for help?"

"He was dead, there was no help for him. And I'd have had to explain what I was doing in the tent in the first place." She shook her head. "I found the pictures stashed in his desk, but I was shaken and in a hurry—I mean, the murderer might have returned at any moment. My scarf must have torn in my rush."

I stood in silence for a moment, thinking over what she'd said. "Prove it."

She grinned and lifted a brow. Then she shrugged and opened a drawer in the desk and pulled out an envelope. She tossed it to me and I jerked, but managed to catch it against my chest. I unfolded the flap and pulled out the photographs inside. They moved magically, more like a short video than a human photograph. I squinted. What was...

"Oh!" I stuffed the photos back in and closed the flap. There had been a lot of flesh and gyrating and I didn't need to see anymore. I tossed the envelope back to her.

"Believe me?"

"For now." I shook my head. "And I don't have any information about that other thing." I gulped. "Which *isn't* a thing, by the way."

"Hank's mistress?"

I wasn't a mistress. I felt my lips purse in anger and willed myself to relax, to not give anything away.

She sighed. "Well, if you think of anything, my offer stands. I'm willing to pay more than you'd imagine for this woman's identity."

Ice shot through my stomach, fear of this information ruining Hank, and my guilt for revealing it, even though it'd been an accident. I backed up, the scarf still in my hand, and left without another word.

10

THE MOON MOVEMENT

I crossed the main square and headed back toward the palace. People milled about, the crowds as thick as ever in the deepening shadows of dusk. Bats dove and flitted overhead and colorful silk and metal lamps sprung to life, one by one, at the many carts and stalls that lined the square.

The crowd thinned in front of the palace, and I hesitated a moment before the main gate. I decided, even though I had cleaned up, to take the back entrance. I figured I had less chance of running into Hank. I knew if I saw him, I'd spill everything, from speaking to Horace, to sneaking into the tent, to accidentally telling Madeline our secret.

I sighed as I stepped into the dark alleyway between the riad and the next building over. The moment she'd latched onto it, I realized the power that information held to cause trouble for Hank. My stomach twisted with guilt. What a weird day it'd been.

As I neared the intersection to the alley that ran behind the riad, a woman in veils passed by, heading away from the palace. She turned for a moment and I recognized her as the servant with the towels who'd spilled on Bernhardt at the feast last night. She jumped when she recognized me and covered her face with her head wrap, then hurried on.

When I reached the back alley, I paused. I could head right, go back to the palace for some dinner and catch up with my friends... or I could follow the servant to the left. The way she looked over her shoulder every few steps and kept to the deep shadows close to the walls made me suspicious. And if I believed Madeline that she hadn't killed Bernhardt, this woman could very well have done it. She'd been there the night of the murder and had some reason to dislike the man. Maybe I could suss out why that was.

I turned left and trailed her, keeping to the shadows and leaving some distance between us. She never entered the main square, but instead stuck to winding alleys and narrow side streets. I trailed her to a dingy bar with neon lettering in a language I didn't understand. Two men leaned against the wall outside the door, smoking, and looked me over as I entered. Inside, music with a heavy bass beat thumped at a deafening volume and bodies packed tightly against each other with barely enough room to stand. I rose on my tiptoes to look over the heads of the crowd and spotted the servant's black veil moving not toward the bar in the back, but to the right, down a hallway.

I sank back down and slowly shouldered my way through the room. By the time I reached the hallway, she'd disappeared. I popped into the ladies' restroom, but found only a young woman I didn't know applying crimson lipstick in the cracked mirror above the sink. All the dingy stalls stood empty. I exited to the hallway and looked around. The only other door led to the men's restroom, and I didn't expect to find her there.

I planted my hands on my hips. Where could she have

gone? Did she know I was following and had given me the slip? I grinned to myself—the slip. I was starting to think of myself as a real investigator. I spotted a symbol that caught my eye and walked to the end of the hallway. Graffiti covered every inch of the wall and even the ceiling.

It was a crescent moon, spray-painted in gold, that made me curious. If I turned my head to just the right angle, the paint seemed to shimmer in the hazy, smoky light. I touched a finger to it and jerked back as a I got a little zap of electricity—magic. I squinted and looked closer and found the outline of a door. The cracks were barely visible in the dim light, camouflaged among the black paint and graffiti.

I pressed on the door, then tried digging my fingers into the crack and pulled. I huffed—it didn't even budge. The symbol might be enchanted to keep the door locked. Too bad my magic skills were lackluster at best. I'd never be able to crack a spell. I'd bet the servant had gone through there. Maybe there was a secret password, or a key, or— I gasped as I remembered the same crescent moon symbol tattooed on her wrist.

If I was better at magic, I could probably spell the symbol onto my own, but instead I patted around my shorts pockets for a pen or marker to draw it on. No such luck. Maybe the bartender had one, but I'd have to fight the crowds.

At that moment, the door to the ladies' room banged open against the wall, and the young woman I'd just seen strode out.

"Hey!"

She looked my way, her lids half closed. "Yeah?"

"Can I borrow your lipstick for a quick sec?"

She handed it to me, but frowned as I used it to draw a half circle on my wrist. She snatched it back and shot me a look as she walked back into the noisy dive bar. I didn't blame her. I probably seemed like a total weirdo. And maybe I was, but this was worth a try.

I walked back to the end of the hallway and glanced back to make sure no one was watching. Then I pressed the hand with the tattoo to the symbol on the door and waited. The gold painted moon shimmered and the panel of wall swung open, revealing a rickety wooden staircase beyond. I grinned, it worked! I stepped inside and the door swung shut behind me and clicked into place. It took my eyes a moment to adjust to the darkness. Voices rose up to me from below, and the damp chilly air brought goose bumps to my bare arms and legs.

"We should celebrate!" A man's deep voice shouted from below and cheers answered him. It sounded like there was quite a crowd. I squinted and carefully navigated the creaky wooden steps down into the cool air of a basement. Footsteps thudded overhead in the bar and the thumping bass sound rattled the few lamps that hung from the low beams of the ceiling. A crowd of at least a hundred huddled together, sitting on overturned buckets and crates of beer. Brooms, mops, and bottles of cleaning supplies stood piled in a corner, and the whole space had a slight smell of bleach. The group of mostly women formed a loose circle. As I moved closer, a few turned to give me a quick glance, then focused again on the center of the circle, where the servant I'd followed now stood.

She raised her arms, her moon tattoo visible. "This is not a victory."

"Bernhardt's dead," a woman shouted from the outer ring of the crowd. "Damn straight it is." More cheers went up.

The servant shook her head and motioned for quiet.

"Who is that?" I whispered to a woman wearing big hoop earrings beside me.

"You new?"

I nodded.

She smirked. "That's Lilya, everyone knows Lilya."

"She big in this, uh—" I racked my brain. What was this? "Organization?"

The woman laughed. "In the Moon Movement? Yeah, she's one of the original fighters for equality."

As the crowd quieted, Lilya continued. "My brother is still imprisoned, merely for holding and publicly expressing dissident views that the government wanted to suppress. So, you tell me. Is this a victory? Bernhardt Beckham may be dead, but Urs Volker has already taken his place."

The crowd grew quieter. "And if Urs goes, there will just be another to replace him. Changing wardens is not enough —we need institutional change!" She pounded a fist into her palm.

"Yeah!" Cries of support rang out from the crowd.

"We need a voice, we need equality, we need rights."

"Yes!" The woman in the gold earrings shouted and raised her fist.

"This movement isn't just about the right to express unpopular opinions anymore. I started it as that, when they took my brother away." Lilya's dark eyes burned with fierceness. "But it's grown. It's about equal rights for women, for shifters, for everyone!"

The basement broke out in cheers.

"I know we all met just last night, so I thank you for making time for this emergency meeting. But I wanted us to come together to reemphasize our values. While others may resort to violence, we will not. And let us not use Bernhardt's death as an excuse to go back on our values."

I nudged the woman next to us. "This is, uh, my first meeting. You guys met last night? Is this where you usually meet?"

She nodded. "We were here last night, yes. The week before we met at another bar. We go where they'll host us. Lilya will tell us where and when the next meeting will be before we leave. We move around to different locations to keep it secret."

I frowned. "So Lilya was here? *All* last night?"

She nodded. "Well, she has a day job, we all do. When she got off she came here—probably around eight o'clock. We were here till after midnight."

Huh. Then she probably hadn't killed Bernhardt, unless she'd snuck back after the meeting. But it took almost an hour by camel to get out to the encampment by the oasis, and then she'd have had to get back into the palace unseen. I supposed she could have done it in the morning, but then that would have put her entering the tent and leaving it in broad daylight. Plus, if she meant what she said, she didn't consider Bernhardt's death to have accomplished much. She may have spilled on him as a way to vent some of her frustration, but that was a far cry from killing him. I sighed. It was still a possibility, but my gut told me Lilya didn't do it. I was back to no suspects at all.

I nudged the woman beside me again. "So... all this secrecy. You'd be in big trouble if you got caught meeting like this?"

She nodded, her eyes wide. "We could be thrown in Carclaustra, like Lilya's brother."

I gulped.

"And you're here too, you know. You're risking just as much as the rest of us, even if you are a foreigner." She looked me up and down.

Guess I did kind of stand out with my bright red hair and pale skin. Suddenly the rattling base beat cut out and Lilya and the rest of us froze. My eyes slid up to the low ceiling. A few sets of footsteps thudded across the floor and a man barked out orders.

The woman beside me hissed a curse. I lifted my brows and she mouthed, "Police." My shoulders bunched up and my stomach clenched in fear. Oh no, I'd really done it this time. If I got arrested and sent to Carclaustra... I shook my head. How could I explain this? And what would happen to Lilya and all the others?

Lilya muttered, "Time to go. Quiet now." We shuffled forward and moved toward the back of the basement, slowly and quietly.

I lifted my brows and the woman beside me whispered, "There's a back way out. We always make sure there is. Someone must have spilled about the meeting."

Knocks thundered against the door at the top of the stairs and the group broke into chaos, forgetting all attempts at silence. Lilya held the metal door at the back of the room ajar and everyone poured out.

CRACK!

I looked back over my shoulder as bodies slammed into me from the right and left, jostling to get out. Booted feet jogged down the rickety stairs into the basement.

"They broke the spell!" a woman screeched.

Panic coursed through me as I was shoved out the door by others behind me into the warm night air. Meeting members fled down the alleyway, to the right and left. Shouts sounded from behind and I froze, panicked.

A strong hand clenched around my upper arm and yanked me hard to the side.

"Come with me," a hoarse voice commanded.

11

A FLY ON THE WALL

I sucked in a huge lungful of air to scream, but when I opened my mouth no sound came out. A low chuckle came from the dark figure who held my arm in a vice and dragged me down a dark alley, away from the shouts and clamor of the bar raid.

"It's a muffling spell." He clicked his tongue. "You should know how to break out of something so simple by now."

I recognized the voice—Horace. The tightness in my chest relaxed. He dashed behind a dumpster and towed me behind. We pressed our backs up against a crumbling plaster wall as officers ran by the mouth of the alley, shouting orders. Once their voices faded, he nodded.

"You can talk again." He lifted a brow. "Just don't scream."

I pressed a few fingertips to my throat. "I didn't know it was you." I blinked up at him. As my eyes adjusted to the dark of the night, his high cheekbones became visible below the shadows of his deep-set eyes. "How did you know where I was?"

He sniffed. "At a meeting for a subversive group?" He gave a slow blink. "I think I'm starting to rub off on you."

I grinned. "I've decided to investigate Bernhardt Beckham's murder. I followed a servant who works at the palace here, I had no idea what the meeting was for." I sighed. "She's not really a suspect anymore, though."

We stood in silence for a few moments. Some rat or other little creature rustled through a pile of litter nearby and the shouts of officers grew more distant.

"Why are you looking into dear Bernie's murder?"

"Ah. I got kicked out of the bakery." I rubbed the back of my neck. "I may have accidentally ruined a bake. It's just been a, a weird time for me, lately. I decided I'd be useful and see what I could suss out." I shrugged. "Instead, I've just ended up almost getting arrested. Oh, and I revealed a secret to a reporter." I sighed and stared down at my booted feet.

Horace said nothing for several long moments. I figured he'd realized what a loser his long-lost sister was.

"Who's your next suspect?"

I looked up in surprise. "Oh. I uh—don't really have one. I thought the journalist did it, then Lilya, the woman who works in the palace. But now I'm not so sure." I shook my head.

"No one comes to mind?"

I swallowed and mulled over what I knew. "Well. When I was in the tent earlier today, I overheard Urs Volker. It seems he's become warden of Carclaustra Prison now. And he said that he'd personally put the protection spells in place around Bernhardt's tent, so he had access and a motive."

Horace folded his arms. "Seems you do have a lead." He swallowed and his Adam's apple bobbed. "When are you going to look into him?"

I choked. "Into Urs Volker? The guy is scary."

Horace lifted one brow ever so slightly. "You're in a dark

alleyway with the number-one most wanted criminal in all the kingdoms, and you're scared of Urs Volker?"

I grinned. "Yeah, but... you're my brother."

He leaned back, his face disappearing into deep shadow so that I couldn't see his expression, but he stayed quiet for several moments.

"Imogen, it's criminal how little you know of your power. Do you want to know how I knew you were here? I followed you." He leaned forward, the dim moonlight barely filtering between the narrow buildings to cast light on the sharp planes of his face. "I am always in disguise. As swallows we are uniquely capable of convincingly and consistently appearing to be something we are not."

In a blink, my brother disappeared and Urs Volker took his place. I gasped and recoiled. I scrambled backward, knocked into a crate, and sent a few mice skittering away. Horace's face returned.

My chest heaved. "You startled me."

"Disguises go beyond what they think we are capable of. What I'm about to show you, you can't tell anyone about it. If you think wearing another's face scares them, how do you think they'd feel about this?"

I wasn't sure who he meant by *they*, but he should probably include me in that group. I'd been frightened by how quickly he turned from my brother into the pale and intimidating Urs Volker.

In a flash, Horace disappeared. My stomach dropped. He hadn't just changed his face this time, he'd erased it, and the rest of him.

"We can go invisible?" I barely breathed the words.

Meow.

I jumped back, startled to find a black cat sitting at my feet, staring up at me. I took a breath, then another. Was this Horace?

Or would I sound completely ignorant to my brother (wherever he was) if I started speaking to an alley cat? I licked my lips.

"Um, hey kitty or... brother?"

The cat nodded.

I gasped and pressed my hands to my mouth. Then I crouched down beside him. "Sea snakes! It's really you?"

Instinctively, I reached a hand out to scratch his head and the cat hissed, revealing needle sharp fangs. I recoiled. "Yeah, it's you." He was almost as scary as Maple and Wiley's shared pet, Cat, who was notably not a cat. They'd left him at home in Bijou Mer with Maple's family. The kids got a kick out of him, and even though her dad shouted about it, he had a soft spot for the little monster.

The hairs on my arms rose, as if by static electricity. I blinked and when I opened my eyes, found myself staring at a pair of man's legs in black pants. I tipped my head up and found Horace looming over me once again. I rose back up to standing tall.

"You hissed at me."

He folded his arms. "I just turned into a cat and that's all you have to say?"

I shook my head. "No. I just don't know what to say. That was incredible." I frowned. "Hank hasn't mentioned that spell."

Horace scoffed. "He probably doesn't know it's possible. Again, this is a secret. It makes us as dangerous and worthy of revulsion as a shifter to them."

Again, the "them."

"I've been able to follow you anywhere, Imogen, undetected."

I looked down and wrapped my arms around myself, not sure if I felt totally comfortable with that.

"It's how I was able to keep you safe tonight."

I looked up and nodded. "Thank you, for that. I don't feel as comfortable wearing a disguise as you do, though, even if it's for good reason."

He lifted a brow. "Even if you could do so to spy on Urs Volker?"

Cold shot through my stomach. "Like pretend to be one of his officers?" I shook my head. "I'd be afraid of getting the accent wrong or that he'd speak German and I wouldn't know how to respond."

Horace groaned. "You're thinking small." He smirked. "Or maybe not small enough."

He disappeared again. In the space his head had just occupied, a fat black horsefly flew in lazy loops and circles, and after a few seconds, Horace reappeared.

My jaw dropped. "You were the fly?"

"You could spy on him. As a fly, a lizard, a mouse—anything you wanted, and go undetected. No German necessary." He gave a short sniff. "Though there's a spell for that too."

I chuckled. "A mouse? My luck, I'd get distracted by cheese and end up stuck in a trap."

Horace leaned against the wall again and leveled me a look. His dark eyes glinted. "Well, the flying creatures are more fun anyway."

"You mean, I could fly?" A huge smile stretched across my face. "I've always wanted to fly."

"I'll teach you." He pushed off the wall.

"Oh." My eyes widened. "You mean... now? Here?"

He shrugged. "A dark alleyway seems like the perfect place to learn some secret magic to me."

I grinned. "Okay." But then, remembering some of my

past lessons with Hank, my stomach sank. "Just to warn you, I'm not the fastest learner."

"I've already given you lessons, remember? In the gypsy wagon."

"Oh, yeah." I glanced down. When I was with Horace, I felt safe. I saw my brother, not the wanted criminal. But that reminder that he'd killed the strongman and taken his place in the carnival filled me with unease. I shifted and bit my lip. Maybe this wasn't such a great idea, spending time with Horace.

"And I beg to differ. You learned quite fast." He shrugged. "If we'd grown up together, I would have taught you all kinds of things."

I swallowed against a lump in my throat. No matter who he was to the rest of the magical world, to me, he was my brother. And learning I was magical, struggling to control my powers, always feeling behind and slower and less able than everyone else around me... it weighed on me, more than I acknowledged. And to have Horace tell me I was powerful and capable—it reminded me how much I'd missed by not growing up with my big brother and my magical birth family. Junie had told me that Horace had carried me around when I was a baby, explaining everything to me. Now was my chance to make up for some of that lost time.

I took a deep breath and nodded. "All right. What do I do first?"

"Find a source of power."

I closed my eyes and nodded. The thumping bass beat of the bar beside us called to me. I drew it in.

"Good. Now imagine being a, hm, a moth. Picture it. But then also imagine being it. You have wings at your back, you're small, the breeze blows you around—try to feel it."

I scrunched my eyes tighter and did as he said. A breeze came up, magic swept around me, and my eyes flew open. "Did I do it?"

Horace gasped and took a step back, his eyes wide.

I blinked. "What?" I looked down at my body. "Oh." I'd half succeeded. Writhing insect legs stuck out of my torso and thick tawny fur blanketed my human arms. I patted my face and poked myself in the eye—one of four eyes it seemed. I looked back at Horace. Well, I'd startled a real reaction out of him. I'd take that as a certain kind of success. I grinned and a long, rolled-up straw thing tumbled out of my mouth.

Horace turned green. "It's worse when you smile." He looked like he might be sick. "Try again."

I chuckled and closed my eyes. It took a few more tries, but I learned more quickly and easily than I'd expected to, and soon had the transformation spell down. I had to admit, Horace was a great teacher. Not that Hank wasn't, I just tended to get distracted by his broad shoulders and sparkling blue eyes.

Horace hired us a couple of camels and we rode out toward the base of Damavash Volcano. It loomed above us, its blue veins pulsing in the dark night sky. Glowing white tents formed the camp that housed Urs and his officers, along with some other wedding guests.

"The tribes are always clamoring for power," Horace explained as we rode. "Some want to maintain some inde-pendence from the city and stay out here. Others believe that by staying in the riad, close to the king, they're be able to have more influence on him."

I frowned as I thought about that rude guy from the feast the night before. "Like Ario Tuk."

He nodded. "King Benam is weak. The tribes, the most

aggressive and vocal of them, are the real power in the kingdom."

We reached the camp and dismounted, leaving our camels to graze on the far side of the oasis pool. We then crept quietly toward the tents. I led Horace to the one that had been Bernhardt's.

"I don't know where Urs's tent is, but it's probably nearby." My voice came out as barely a whisper, but Horace nodded that he'd heard. We moved through the camp. A shadow passed across the canvas of a tent at my right. I froze until the creak of springs signaled that the person inside had gone to bed. The light flicked out a moment later. I let out the breath I'd been holding. Soon we spotted a ring of tents with a picnic table situated in the center. Several men in black military uniforms sat at the table, eating out of tin plates and playing a dice game.

Horace lifted his chin toward them, his full lips pressed together. "My guess is Urs is in the one they keep glancing toward."

I frowned. I hadn't noticed anything like that. I watched more closely. Sure enough, one of the men rolled the dice, then threw his fists in the air and bellowed something in German. His friend slapped his arms down and they all glanced to the left of the circle, toward a tent lit up from within by shifting gold firelight.

I sniffed and shook my head at Horace in amazement. "You see everything, don't you?"

"More than most, maybe." He flashed his eyes at me. "You're up."

I hesitated a moment, then jumped. "Oh. Right." Nerves raced through me, and I shivered. Okay. I could do this.

"Focus, Imogen."

I closed my eyes and took a few deep breaths. I sensed

energy coming from the breeze that blew through the desert valley and made the tent fabric snap. I drew from it, imagined what I wanted to become, and—whoosh!

I felt as though I'd been caught in a whirlwind, then suddenly spit out. Everything was different. I hovered midair, my tiny moth wings fluttering as my six legs dangled beneath me. I did a quick loop-de-loop. Horace was right, flying was amazing. I rose up in the air to Horace's height, where his giant pale blue eyes took up the entire horizon.

"Go. And Imogen... be careful."

I hesitated. He wasn't coming with me? I'd just assumed he would.

"I can't enter that tent, for reasons I won't go into just now. But go, you'll do fine." Horace stared at me. "And remember—focus."

Right. I had to keep pulling energy from the breeze, or whatever source I chose, to fuel the transformation. If I lost my concentration and stopped, I'd turn back into myself, or maybe that weird moth-human hybrid version of myself. I took a deep breath and fluttered away. I spun and twirled and bobbed on the breeze, feeling light and free. I landed on the side of the tent and rubbed my front legs together, cleaning them and the bristly hairs that covered my body. It was strange, how my mind seemed to be human, and yet some moth instincts seemed to come with the package. And lucky for me, too, because a moment later I sensed a change in the air. I launched and took flight, narrowly avoiding the giant bat that swooped overhead and barely missed me.

In my head, I screamed as I zipped to the tent flaps and darted inside. I looped right, then dipped down, and finally arced to the wall opposite the entrance and landed on the canvas of the tent. My tiny heart pounded as I caught my breath. That had been close. Not that the coast was clear now. I shuffled and spotted Urs Volker at his desk. We'd guessed right. Only a pen, calendar, and one stack of papers, all at right angles to each other, interrupted the open plain of the desktop. Everything, from the perfect corners on his bedsheets to the straight part of Urs's hair, screamed order and discipline. A fountain pen magically scratched away at a piece of paper.

A low voice spoke from outside and Urs barked, "Enter." The pen stopped and hovered in midair.

An officer in a black uniform ducked into the tent, then stood before Urs with his shoulders squared.

"Yes?" Urs prompted.

"Varden Volker. Za medical examiner's report." The officer handed over a manila folder.

Urs opened it and pulled out some papers. A line formed between his brows and he rubbed his hand over his mouth. He read aloud as his eyes skimmed the report. "Shtrangled to death... crushed trachea." Urs shook his head. "Characteristic damage from oon choke holdt. Somevone used hees own fighting technique against him."

"Sir?" The officer hesitated, then spoke again. "Somevone trained een your technique killt him?" He took a sharp intake of air. "Vone of us?"

Urs didn't answer for a moment. A burst of laughter from the men playing dice outside interrupted the tense silence. Then he looked up at the officer. "Zis doesn't leaf zis tent, ees zat understoodt?"

"Couldn't eet haf been magic?" the officer tried.

Urs shook his head. "I put za security shpells een place myself. Hee had an emergency shpell, one zat negated anyvone from using magic een hees room besides heemself or I. I checked za scene and found he had deployt it, meaning somevone used zer bare hands to keel heem."

A choke hold? I pictured Madeline L'Orange or Lilya trying to choke Bernhardt out and it didn't fit. They were both slender and small, and would probably have a hard time even getting their arms around his thick neck. This had to be a man then... or someone strong and deadly enough to overpower the large and highly trained Beckham. Urs seemed guiltier than ever and I flushed with gratitude toward Horace for teaching me how to transform and encouraging me to trust my ability to do so. What a natural big brother. I'd have to tell him so once I got out of here, even though he'd probably feel uncomfortable with the compliment. I grinned to myself. He'd just have to get used to it. Whoops! I caught my mind drifting and remembered Horace's words. I needed to focus, to be one with the moth.

The men spoke a few more words, and then the officer turned to go, dismissed. As he ducked out, Urs called to him, "And close za flaps on za vay out."

"Da, Varden Volker."

Sea snakes! I had to get out of here before they sealed me in. I pushed off the tent fabric and flew across the open air of the tent as quickly as I could, but the officer had already stepped out.

"Veinhardt!" Urs barked.

The officer stepped back inside immediately and stood at attention.

"Get zat disgusting insect out off here." He waved a hand in dismissal and I realized he was talking about me. I flew on as quickly as I could and as the officer swiped at me, I dodged and ducked out of the tent and into the cool night air. I breathed a sigh of relief as I zipped away, until I sensed another diving bat headed straight for me. I dodged and swerved, but it moved with me, zipping between the tents, its squeaks and screeches deafening.

The bat closed in on me and my heart raced in panic until I reached the oasis. Just as I sensed the bat a millimeter behind me, I squeezed my eyes shut and visualized becoming myself, my real human self, with all my might. Midair, the tornado of magic caught me up, spun me around, and dumped me out as my human self. I dropped through the air until my feet hit the ground. I stumbled forward, slammed into something, then fell to a crumpled heap in the soft sand. I lay there, panting. The lap of the water against the shore met my ears, and I spotted the killer bat spiraling up and away into the night sky. I squinted. *Francis? That you?*

"You made it out alive."

I rolled to my side and found Horace beside me, sprawled on his back. I sat up quickly and shook his shoulder. "Are you all right? What happened?"

His eyes flashed. "You knocked me over."

"I did?" I pressed a hand to my chest and breathed a sigh of relief to have human hands again. Then I realized what had happened. "The thing I slammed into, was you?"

He stared at me, expressionless. My first instinct was to apologize, but then my adrenaline crashed and I realized how close I'd come to being eaten alive. I chuckled and his eyes widened. I shook my head. "I'm sorry, I don't mean to laugh, but—" I chuckled again, then laughed, then burst into giggles. "I was flying away from a bat," I gasped out between fits of laughter. I buried my face in my hands. When I peeked between my fingers I found Horace staring up at the stars, his hands behind his head. I cleared my throat and vowed to calm down. I rolled to my back and looked up, listening to the soft lapping of the water.

Horace broke the easy silence between us. "It's strange, not being alone after so long."

I swallowed.

"I like it."

Warmth spread through my chest, but I sniffed. "Oh come on. You've got a whole army, you're not alone... are you?" I looked sideways at him.

He lay quiet for a moment, then smirked. "They're all a bunch of yes-men, it feels like talking to myself." His eyes shifted to me. "This is better."

12

SLOW HANDS

I hustled through the halls of the palace, skirting by busy servants. The whole place was in a tizzy as the household prepared for the wedding tomorrow. The garlands of lilies, roses, and jasmine hung over the railing into the courtyard and the servants scurrying about with piles of wrapped presents made it hard not to think about Hank's impending marriage. And I was trying really hard. I attempted to catch someone's eye to ask directions to the bakery, but no one paid me any attention.

I'd gotten in late last night and Maple, K'ree, and Annie were already sleeping. Iggy had opted to sleep in the oven with the other baking fires apparently, so I slid into bed and pulled the mosquito netting shut around me without a chance to speak to any of my friends. I lay there for a while before I fell asleep, thinking over Bernhardt's death. If Urs was guilty, it was going to be difficult to prove, and I'd have to make sure I had hard evidence. Urs himself had admitted that the protective spells had allowances for both him and Bernhardt, making Urs one of the only people with the ability to use magic against him. But Bernhardt hadn't been killed with magic. Had Urs killed him in that way because using magic would have turned suspicion on him?

On the camel ride back to the city last night, Horace had explained what the warden had meant by "emergency spell." The Air Kingdom was full of innovators and inventors, they loved to mix technology and magic. And apparently they manufactured little boxes that stored spells for deployment in an emergency setting. Bernhardt's had ensured that the murderer's magical powers were disabled in the tent, which should have given Bernhardt an advantage, except that this person was both strong and had military training in hand-to-hand combat.

Horace also explained what Urs had likely meant when I overheard him at the crime scene saying one of his spells would have made an intruder violently ill. The Air Kingdom had perfected the use of charms for holding spells. Some existed that, if hung over a doorway (or an entrance to a tent), would cause anyone who entered without permission to become ill or suffer some terrible fate. The charm required magical charging daily, but it was effective protection.

No matter how hard I thought, the pieces wouldn't come together, and I eventually drifted off to sleep. I'd awoken about half an hour ago and found a note on my nightstand from Maple, telling me that she'd talked to Amelia and gotten her to lift my ban from the bakery. I'd been elated, then horrified to find it was nearly midmorning and I was hours late for work. Of course, my boss was Maple so I wasn't too worried about getting in trouble, but I felt anxious to see my friends. So much had happened yesterday, and while I wasn't sure how much I was ready to share, especially about meeting with Horace, I craved the comfort of talking some of it over with Maple and Iggy.

Only now, again, I was lost. I stopped and turned around. Which was the back of the riad? As I wondered, someone passed by and shoulder clipped me, hard. I lurched forward.

"Ow!" I rubbed my arm and turned to find Ario Tuk, the chauvinistic idiot from the wedding feast, glaring at me. No wonder he'd hit me, his shoulders were as wide as half the hallway. A thin red cut ran the length of his left cheek, through his beard. I cocked my head to the side—wonder where he got that?

"Apologize."

I lifted my brows. *"You* ran into *me."*

"You were standing in my way!"

It was my turn to glare, but he didn't notice. He was too busy smoothing his white robes down with his enormous, thick hands. "Well, since you've thrown yourself in my path, I've been looking for a servant to bring me some food. Time to stop standing around and do your job." He lifted his thick brows. "Well. What are you waiting for? I want breakfast in my room in five."

I planted my hands on my hips. "No." For so many reasons, but I decided to give him the most pertinent. "It's not my job." I turned to go, though I still had no idea where the bakery was. Then I paused and spun on my heel. "And I pity the person whose job it is." I jabbed my finger at him.

His face darkened and he seemed to puff up bigger. "Disobedient and lippy! I have never experienced such rude servants. Were this my family's palace, I guarantee you'd not only be fired, but hanged."

Oh wow. This guy was unlikely to be voted boss of the year.

"And my guy is sick." Ario's lip curled in disgust. "I can't wait until he's feeling better and I don't have to deal with subpar servants like you. I'm docking extra from his pay for the inconvenience."

I shook my head and trembled with anger. What a jerk. Docking his servant's pay for being ill? Like he'd gotten sick on purpose. I sniffed. Just dealing with Ario day in and day out would make me ill.

Before I could spout something off that I'd likely later regret, Shaday swept up in a flowing red gown, her black hair gathered in a long, wavy ponytail down her back, and huge gold hoops glinting in her ears.

"Imogen." She dipped her chin in a nod at me. I curtsied back and let out a shaky breath. Her gaze swung to Ario and her tone flattened. "Ario."

His face slid into an overly cheerful grin, his teeth flashing white against his thick black beard. "Princess Shaday, what a pleasure to see you."

Her eyes narrowed.

"Don't let me hold you up. You must be busy preparing for the big day tomorrow." He bowed and I lifted a brow in surprise—shocking that with all those muscles on muscles he was actually able to bend over. He stood and backed away. "Best of luck for tomorrow."

Once he'd turned his back, Shaday gave a slight shake of her head, which for her was as good as an eye roll and a heavy sigh.

"He wanted my hand, you know. I'm assuming he's trying a new tactic, being polite."

I raised my brows.

Shaday stepped closer and lowered her voice. Only a couple of servants moved about at the ends of the hallway, far enough away to be out of earshot. "He hounded my father relentlessly."

"He must have a big crush."

She gave me a flat look. "On the throne. He wants to be future ruler of the Fire Kingdom, I'm pretty sure he despises me. But that doesn't keep him from still trying to get with me every chance he can."

"Still?" My mouth dropped open when she nodded. "That's terrible."

"He's been quite... forceful in his approach." Her mouth tightened and she balled her hands into fists. "I had to teach him some manners."

My eyes opened wide in shock. I eyed the many rings on her fingers—pointy rings. That probably explained the cut on Ario's cheek, but I had a hard time seeing Shaday being violent, even to slap someone who deserved it. Then again, some of those moves she'd done the other day looked more like martial arts than dance.

Shaday shrugged one slim shoulder and brought me back to the present. "It's part of the reason I finally agreed to an engagement to Hank. He's much preferable to the alternative."

My stomach twisted and Shaday's dark eyes widened. "My apologies, Imogen, that was unthinking of me. I only meant if I have to be married, it's good that it be to someone kind and with brain cells. I would not have been so lucky if my father had relented to Ario. But many of the Fire Kingdom tribes are unhappy that I'm being married to someone from outside the kingdom." She lifted a slim brow. "Difficult to please everyone, and my own preferences are apparently at the bottom of the list, even at my own wedding."

I sighed and shook my head. "I'm sorry. That's a lot weighing on you."

"There you are."

We turned to find Shaday's mother striding toward us. It was easy to see where Shaday got her elegance and grace.

Shaday dipped into a curtsy. "Mother."

I curtsied low and dropped my eyes to the queen's gold-sandaled feet. "Queen Ranita."

I rose to find her staring at her daughter, her hands folded in front of her long, gold dress. "I've sent several servants to find you, but eventually called them off since we're so short-staffed and came to look myself. Where *have* you been?"

Shaday blinked a few times. "Just strolling the palace, as I often do, for exercise."

I tried to keep a poker face. After the feats I'd seen her perform yesterday, I doubted strolling the palace would be much of a workout for her, no matter how maze-like it was.

"Muma sneezed this morning."

Shaday held still but the corner of her mouth twitched ever so slightly. "Is this what you sent the servants to tell me?"

Queen Ranita leveled her daughter a hard look. "Don't jest. Your wedding is tomorrow and I am not risking you falling ill, could you imagine?" She sniffed and pursed her lips. "It'd be an absolute disaster. So I quarantined Muma with the others."

"Mother!" Shaday's chest heaved. "She's been my nurse since I was a child. I need her."

Ranita lifted a slim finger. "No back talk, this wedding is too important." Shaday stayed silent, but I could tell it took effort. Ranita continued. "Since she will be unable to do your henna, I've had to call in another and I need you in the—"

"No." Shaday's dark eyes were wide.

The queen's lip curled. "No?"

Shaday licked her lips. "I meant no, that won't be necessary, because Imogen here will do it." She swept her slender arms toward me.

I froze, but wished more than anything to bolt, especially as Ranita slid her gaze to me. Her brows pulled down in doubt. "Her?"

"Me?" I echoed.

Shaday nodded once. "Yes. *Won't you*, Imogen?"

"Uh." I had no idea how to do henna but Shaday was silently pleading with me. "Yeah. I will." I gulped.

Ranita stepped closer to me. "Are you sick? Have you been feeling well? Do you have any experience with wedding henna?"

Behind the queen, Shaday's eyes were fixed with laser focus on me, her lips pressed tight together.

"I, uh." I licked my lips, unsure how to answer. "I'm feeling perfectly healthy, Queen Ranita, and I'm sure Shaday has a reason for putting her confidence in my henna skills." Didn't she? Because as far as I knew, I didn't have any.

The queen gave me another once-over, then turned to her daughter. "You need to be ready by noon. We're having a run through and need you to mark positions after lunch." With that, she spun around, her skirt whirling around her ankles, and strode away the way she'd come.

I blinked at Shaday. "What just happened?"

Her lips quirked to the side. "I always wonder the same thing after speaking to my mother."

I chuckled. Then groaned. "Look, I want to help, but I have no idea how to do what you're asking me to."

Shaday smiled, tight-lipped. "Don't worry. It'll be just like frosting a cake."

I followed her down the hallway. "Somehow, I doubt that very much."

"Ha!" She threw her head back and laughed—just laughed, like a normal person. That made twice I'd seen her laugh now, in all the months I'd known her. I shook my head. She was such a mystery.

"Okay, you were right." I scooted closer on my little round pouf and turned Shaday's slender hand. "This is a lot like frosting a cake." I grinned. "It's kinda fun."

We sat in the private walled garden off her suite. The trickle of water from the central fountain and the chirping of the birds that flitted from tree to tree made for pleasant background noise. A breeze blew the scent of honeysuckle to me and I sighed happily.

"Thank you for filling in for Muma." A little crease formed between her brows. "I hope she's feeling all right and that my mother is just irrationally worried."

I nodded. "Me, too." I used the squeeze bottle of reddish brown ink to form a vine over the back of Shaday's golden brown hand, then added little leaves.

"You know, it'd be easier to enchant the bottle to do it." Shaday's gentle eyes twinkled.

"For you, maybe. I'm still getting the swing of this magic stuff." I looked up. "Wait, you could just enchant it to do it for you?"

She shook her head. "I'd still have to tell it what designs to do." She lifted her eyes to the sky. "I have no artistic talent."

I opened my mouth to protest that she was a beautiful dancer, then promptly shut it. She didn't know I'd been accidentally spying on her. "Well, then, you'll have to put up with me doing it the manual way."

I trailed a line of thick ink to the edge of her hand, then gently turned her wrist, bringing her hand palm up.

She jerked. "Wait, I should—"

I froze.

"Warn you," she finished lamely.

My mouth hung open. Thick calluses covered much of her hand, but blisters at the base of her fingers bled and a streak of raw, pink burn stretched across the whole of her palm. I looked up and my stomach twisted as I imagined the pain of these injuries.

"This is why you wanted me to do the henna, you didn't want a stranger to see this?"

Shaday swallowed and her nostrils flared.

I scooted closer, gently holding her wrist. "Shaday, Maple's a lot better at healing spells. She could fix the blisters and the—"

"The blisters will turn to calluses." Shaday let out a shaky breath. "And I need my calluses."

I searched her face, worried for her. How had she done this to her hands? Was it from dancing with fire? That would explain the burns, maybe the calluses, too. Or could it have been from a skirmish? Urs mentioned that Bernhardt's killer had likely been cut by his star medal. I shook the thought out of my head.

"I can't tell you why I need them," she continued. "Imogen, please don't say anything. To anyone."

I blew out a heavy breath. "Would you like me to cover them up?"

She nodded. "Yes. Please."

I worked on for a time more, both of us quiet. Shaday was definitely a lot more hard-core than I'd thought, and more secretive, too. Could she have had something to do with Bernhardt's death? She was skilled and strong. But why? Had she done it for Elke? Did they do it together? I jumped when she eventually broke the silence.

"How are you doing, Imogen?"

"Oh, good." I wiped my forehead with the back of my hand. It was another sunny day, and warm out in the garden. "I'm almost done with the second hand, actually."

"No, I meant, how are you, in general?"

I glanced up at her.

"This can't be easy, doing wedding henna for the woman your love is going to marry." She shrugged a shoulder. "I almost wish I hadn't asked you to do it, but you're quite good, so I'm glad I did."

I gave her a little smile. "It's not your fault—actually, you've been lovely about everything." I let out a little sigh. "It's not an easy situation, but it is what it is."

Shaday made a noise in the back of her throat. "That's an understatement. Elke's having a difficult time of it."

I finished the last stroke, then looked up from working on the henna design. "Elke? Why wouldn't she be happy for you?"

Shaday parted her lips to speak, then promptly clamped her mouth shut again.

I rolled my eyes at myself. "Her father was murdered yesterday. Of course she's having a hard time right now." I set the squeeze bottle of henna down on the table next to us, beside our orange blossom lemonades. "All done. What do you think?"

She quirked her lips to the side and held up her hands. "Beautiful."

As she admired her hands, I thought about Shaday. She had a lot of secrets... though I supposed we all had some. Mine involved hanging out with a wanted inter-kingdom criminal who happened to be my brother, but I was sure she had some big ones, too.

13

SUSPICION

S haday walked me back to the bakery. She pointed out oil paintings and right and left turns so that I wouldn't get lost again. I nodded and smiled but knew, deep down, that I'd *definitely* get lost again. We said our goodbyes and she went to go sit for portraits with my boyfriend, or something, while I went to help make his wedding cake. Totally normal situation.

"Well, look who finally decided to grace us with her presence." Iggy peeked out of the recessed wall oven. "Was that your soon-to-be sister wife I spotted with you?"

I rolled my eyes. K'ree plucked my apron off the hook and handed it to me. I smiled my thanks and looped it over my head, then tied the strings behind me as I stood beside Maple at the work station.

"We missed you yesterday." Maple pouted and nudged my shoulder with her own. "I'd give you a hug, but—" She waved her frosting-stained hands at me, a piping bag in one. "Are you mad at me? For sending you out?"

I shook my head and grinned at her. "No. I mean, I missed being here with you guys." I sighed. "But it was probably a good call." I scanned the pile of purple frosting flowers scattered about on wax paper. "These for the wedding cake?"

Maple nodded and Sam blinked his milky baby blues at me. "Doesss that upssset you, Imogen?" His narrow shoulders sagged.

I winked and waved a hand. "Naw. I'm good, but thanks, Sam. That's very kind of you to ask."

He blushed from his collar to his forehead.

Maple leaned close and spoke in my ear. "I needed you yesterday."

I grimaced. "Was it bad?"

She gave a tight nod.

I winced. "Wiley and Wool?"

She nodded emphatically.

I threw my arm around her shoulders and gave her a squeeze. "I'll try to help diffuse the tension and keep them from going at each other's throats."

Maple's blue eyes widened. "You don't understand, they're—"

At that moment, Wiley and Wool strode toward us, coming from the direction of the wall of spices and dry ingredients. Wool said something and Wiley threw his head back and laughed, a deep belly laugh. My eyes slid to Maple, then right back to the guys. I swear, I could count all of Wiley's molars. He wiped tears from his eyes, then clapped Wool on the back and kept his arm around his shoulders the rest of the way to our work station.

"Oh man. The snake was in the basket! Ha!" Wiley shook his head. "You're killing me, man."

"You kidding?" Wool nudged Wiley with his elbow and turned to the rest of us bakers gathered around the worktable. "How do you work with this funny man? I'd have tears pouring into my batter. I'd have to constantly remake everything."

Annie gave him a flat look. "We somehow manage."

I shot a sideways glance at Maple. "What is this?"

She shrugged and wrung her hands in her apron, wiping off the frosting with quick, rough motions. "I have no idea."

K'ree giggled. "No one can figure it out. Annie thinks it's some kind of act. Yann thinks Wiley's snapped and lost it."

I nodded. "Yeah. Could be both."

"Well, better get back to my batter." Wool jerked his curly-haired head toward the Fire Kingdom's station.

"Back to your batter." Wiley grinned and nodded. "I'm going to start saying that

Wool stuck his hand out, then Wiley smirked and did the same.

"Okay. Seriously, what is happening now?"

K'ree grabbed my arm. "This is the best part, they've made up their own handshake."

Iggy's hysterical, cackling laughter sounded from the oven.

My bottom lip quavered as I fought between bursting into laughter and sympathizing with Maple, who watched in wide-eyed horror. The two men slapped their hands back and forth, shook, gripped wrists, pulled each other into a chest bump, and grabbed each other by the back of the neck. They grinned and stared in each other's eyes.

I folded my arms across my chest. "Well, Maple, I think you've officially been kicked out of the love triangle."

Wool turned to go, then stopped and turned back to Maple. He flashed her a stunning white smile, and his dark eyes sparkled. "Before I forget... Maple, I've been meaning to ask you something. Would you like to get dinner with me tonight? There's this amazing bakery I want to show you. I thought we could go for dessert, after."

Her cheeks flushed bright pink. "Oh. Like a work thing? Scope out some baked goods?"

He pressed his full lips together. "I was hoping it'd be a date."

I looked between them... several times. Maple appeared to be frozen. I nudged her shoulder and muttered, "He's waiting for an answer."

Wiley frowned, then plastered on a smile. He clapped Wool on the back. "Of course she wants to go on a date. Right?" He lifted his brows at her. "I mean, look at the guy. Who wouldn't?"

It was true. Wool was tall, dark, and handsome. And he could bake, was mature, and gave Maple his grandma's top-secret recipe. He was a total dreamboat.

Maple swallowed. Her eyes darted to Wiley, then back to Wool. "Uh, sure. Yes. That sounds—" I lifted a brow as she searched for words. "It sounds really amazing."

Wool's smile had dropped slightly, but he nodded and his lips quirked to the side. "Great. I'll come by your room at seven thirty, then?"

Maple nodded.

Wool smiled. "I look forward to it." He turned and moved to the other side of the kitchen to work with the other Fire Kingdom bakers. Sam, K'ree, Annie, and Yann's faces all swung to Maple and she dipped her chin, her eyes glued to her work. Her pale cheeks burned bright red. Wiley kept his eyes down too. After a few moments, everyone gradually returned to what they were doing, but Annie moved past us a moment later and winked at Maple, then K'ree squeezed her arm and squealed, and Yann gave a thumbs-up. Sam tried a double thumbs-up but used his index fingers.

"This is so embarrassing," Maple hissed as I filled up my piping bag to make sugar flowers. We'd then enchant them to bloom and flutter their petals in an imaginary wind.

I nodded. "Yeah, it's pretty awkward. But hey, at least they didn't start a fist fight over you."

"At least." She grinned.

"And you'll have a great time with Wool. He's such a gentleman, and easy to talk to, even for you."

"Hey!" She looked up, indignant. "I just get nervous around him."

I nodded. "A good sign. Just give him a chance."

She sighed. "Thanks, Imogen, I will." Her eyes darted to Wiley, then back down at the purple pansy she formed. "You think... everyone's okay with us going out?"

"Don't worry about everyone. Everyone seems to have a man crush on your date."

Maple lifted her big eyes up at me. "Imogen, I missed you so much yesterday. You always make me feel better."

"Aw, I missed you, too." I sighed. "A lot."

"Really, did you have a tough day, too? What did you do?"

I froze, not sure how much to tell her.

Maple rolled her eyes. "Duh. I'm so sorry, what a dumb question. Of course you had a rough day. Hank's getting married tomorrow."

I let out a little breath of relief. "No, don't be sorry, it's fine." I tilted my head to the side. "But that was only half of it." I lowered my voice and scooched closer. "Amelia took me back out to the camp where we had the feast and I decided, since I was bored and lonely, to investigate Bernhardt Beckham's death. I snuck into his tent."

Maple's jaw dropped and she looked furtively around. "Imogen. You could get into big trouble." She scoffed. "One day out of the bakery and you're skulking around crime scenes."

I grinned. "You make me sound like a delinquent."

"Well."

My jaw dropped. "Hey!"

She shook her head. "No! I mean, well... what did you find out? Any prime suspects?"

I tried to give her a quick recap, about how at first I'd suspected Madeline L'Orange because I'd seen her and Bernhardt fighting. I explained how I'd traded her a secret for her own secret about Bernhardt blackmailing her with the photos.

Maple clapped her hands to her mouth. She'd forgotten about the frosting on her fingers and left a big blue streak across her cheek. "Oh no. So now this woman knows about you and Hank?"

I shook my head. "No. She just suspects Hank has someone, but she doesn't know who." I frowned. "I just keep hoping that she assumes she interpreted my reaction wrong and doesn't look into it." Wishful thinking, at best.

Maple bit her lip. "Then what?"

I filled her in on following Lilya to the underground (literally) meeting and getting chased out by the police. I left out the part about Horace—all the parts about Horace, actually. I couldn't tell her in the kitchen... and part of me wondered about telling her at all. She only knew Horace as a killer, number-one enemy of the state. She didn't know him like I did.

"So Lilya had an alibi then? She left the feast and got to the meeting and was there till late in the night?"

I nodded. "She could've gone back later to kill him, but...."

"It's pretty far and the way she was talking didn't seem like she was celebrating his death."

I nodded. "That's exactly what I thought."

"So who are you thinking now?" Maple looked around as if the killer might be in the room with us.

"I, uh, I think Urs Volker is likely."

Her blonde brows lifted and I caught K'ree leaning closer, though she kept her eyes down, pretending not to overhear. "Bernhardt's number two in command?"

I nodded. "He's number one now—took the position of warden when Bernhardt died. So he has a strong motive. And he's the one who cast all the security spells that conveniently had no effect on Bernhardt or him."

"Who's to say he cast security spells at all?" Maple shook her head and formed another blue petal. "He had Bernhardt's trust, he could've come in whenever he wanted to, to kill him."

I nodded. "And he was killed by a choke hold, a signature move from their style of hand-to-hand combat. It was someone they'd trained."

Maple's jaw dropped. "Or the trainer himself."

I grinned. She was getting really into this.

"How'd you find this out?" K'ree's eyes widened. "Sorry, I couldn't help but overhear."

"Even I couldn't help but overhear," Iggy called from the oven. "We're all like two feet away from each other."

Annie grinned and nodded at the other end of the table. Fair enough.

"Yeah, though." Maple blinked. "How *did* you find that out? You're becoming quite the detective."

I visualized flying through the air dodging bats and working with Horace on my magic. "Uh...I overheard it."

Once everyone had returned to their work, I dropped my

voice to the quietest whisper I could and felt sure that no one else could hear me. "Maple. I'm starting to suspect someone else though."

She lifted her brows in question.

"Shaday, or really, Shaday and Elke."

Maple gasped. "No. I thought you liked Shaday?"

I nodded. "I do, a lot actually. But I accidentally saw her and Elke together in a storage room yesterday." I filled her in on the dancing and everything since. "Shaday's strong and Elke is trained in Bernhardt's style of fighting. She looked miserable the other night at the feast. Maybe Bernhardt was going to make her go back home to the Air Kingdom with him or something. Shaday and Elke are really close, even Madeline commented on it. Or maybe they just had a bad father-daughter relationship. From what I've seen, Bernhardt wasn't above blackmailing a woman he had a relationship with—doesn't seem like a great guy."

"Huh." Maple's brow wrinkled as she thought it over. "But really, Shaday? She's so tranquil and elegant."

"I know." I shook my head. "But you should've seen her move. I've never seen anything like it. She's hiding a lot."

"What are you going to do?" A wax paper square turned magically while Maple piped a flower on top of it.

"While I was doing her henna earlier, she mentioned seeing Elke tonight. I think they're going to be back in that storage room. I'm going to watch them from behind the hidden screen and see if they admit to killing him to each other."

Maple blinked and blew out a breath. "Wow. I mean, if it's true, Elke would have killed her own father in cold blood, and Shaday would have helped—a princess. This is a big deal, Imogen."

I nodded and my stomach twisted with nerves. It would

have huge implications, and not just for Shaday and Elke, but for me, too. If Shaday was a killer and I exposed her, the wedding would be off, and Hank and I might have a chance to be together. I had to get this right.

"I'm coming with you." Maple nodded. "When should we go?"

I grinned. "No, you're not. You've got a date, remember?"

Her face fell. "Oh. Yeah."

"Try not to act too excited."

"I am excited. It's just...." She whimpered. "I'm afraid I'll do something dumb. He's just so...perfect."

Wiley muttered something and I turned, but he didn't look up. It'd sounded like he'd said, "You are, too."

14

SHADAY AND ELKE

A fter I helped Maple curl her hair into loose waves and I put the last pat of powder on her nose, she left on her date with Wool. She'd had to spell her armpits dry twice before she answered the door. The girl was a bundle of nerves.

Annie leaned over on the bed to catch sight of Wool as the door swung shut. "If I were thirty years younger...."

I helped Iggy climb into a black lantern and waved goodbye to K'ree and Annie. "We're off for an evening stroll."

Annie looked up from the book she sat reading in bed. "We overheard you earlier. Good luck spying on Shaday."

I planted a hand on my hip. "There are no secrets around here, are there?"

K'ree shook her head. "I'd come with, but I want to hear all about Maple's date when she gets back."

I grinned. "We'll hopefully be back by then."

She nodded. "If you don't get arrested."

"Quite the votes of confidence." I shook my head.

K'ree and Annie muttered their goodbyes without looking up. Once the door had shut behind me, I held Iggy up and looked left, then right. Flames sprung to life in lanterns and wall sconces up and down the hallway as dusk deepened into night.

"Right. Where to, then?" Iggy rubbed his little flame hands together.

"That's a good question...."

~

THIRTY MINUTES later we were still wandering the palace, hopelessly lost. I came to the end of a hallway.

"Now, this looks familiar."

"Erk!" Iggy shrieked. "Of course it does. We passed through here five minutes ago."

"We did?" I frowned as I stared at the vase that sat in the alcove up ahead. "I mean, yeah, we did."

Iggy narrowed his eyes at me. "You don't remember. Which way do we go then?"

"Uh." I stepped to the right.

"Nope! We just went right and it led us in a big circle right back here." He sighed. "If we get lost for days and starve, I *will* eat you."

"Wow." I headed left. "I can tell you really missed me yesterday."

"You're the one who left *me* behind."

I lifted my brows. "Would you have wanted to come with me? I mean, I did get banished from the bakery. Not like I left you behind to go on vacation."

"Imogen, you know how I feel. I'm a baking fire, it's what I do, but I don't really fit in with the other flames anymore." He sighed. "I've seen the world and it's changed me."

I bit my lip to hold in my chuckle. "Well, I'll keep that in mind next time I'm banished."

We passed an enormous potted fern and I hesitated. Now that looked familiar... but was it just because I'd already passed by it earlier tonight?

"Tell me everything you saw. I've been stuck in an oven while you were gallivanting about Calloon."

"Er...." I hesitated. I still hadn't told him or Maple or anyone about seeing Horace—not once, but twice yesterday. I was saved from having to answer when I pulled up short in front of an enormous hanging rug. "This is it!" I grinned at Iggy. "I found it."

He gave me flat look and slow clapped.

"Okay, shush." I held a finger to my lips. I shuttered his lamp so that only a sliver of his light peeked out. Then I lifted a side of the heavy rug and ducked into the dark room behind it. It took a few moments and a lot of blinking for my eyes to adjust to the light, but when they did I spotted Shaday and Elke on the other side of the carved wooden screen. I grinned. I'd been right that they were practicing tonight.

Several lit candles sat atop tables and bookshelves draped in tarps, and a large lantern burned beside Elke's feet. She stood, stopwatch in one hand and a notebook in her other, and watched Shaday dance. The princess leapt across the long room, a burning veil between her hands. She twirled and spun the veil around her waist, then overheard, then low again. The curtain of flame burned bright spots into my eyes, so that even when I blinked I saw an after-image of it. Shaday twirled the roaring veil to one arm and held it like a matador. She marched the length of the room, the fire lighting up her dark eyes with a red glow. She did one final spin, threw the veil into the air, then let it float to the ground, where it lay smoldering.

Elke's stopwatch beeped. "That was good. Really good."

She jotted down some notes in her book.

Shaday stalked over to her.

"I think those improvements I made to the fabric really—"

Shaday stopped in front of her, quite close and interrupted her. "You're a cracking genius." Shaday took Elke's face in her hands and roughly kissed her.

I gasped and put a hand to my mouth. Oh. They were *really* good friends.

I held Iggy aloft by my head. He cocked his head to the side as the kiss turned tender and Elke snaked her arms around Shaday's middle. I turned away, aware suddenly of how much we were intruding.

"You and Maple don't act like that." Iggy blinked slowly.

"They're together...a couple," I hissed.

Iggy's mouth formed a perfect O, his eyes opening wide. Then his usual smirk returned and he chuckled. "I know, you dummy."

I rolled my eyes. "We should leave," I whispered.

"Why, because they're kissing?" Iggy frowned. "Maybe Elke's dad found out and tried to break them up, maybe they killed him to keep their secret." He shrugged. "If anything, this just thickens the plot. Don't chicken out now. You don't want Hank marrying a murderer, do you?"

A chill shocked through my chest. I hadn't thought of it like that. Hank being in danger made me more afraid than if I myself were in jeopardy. I nodded. "You're right." I turned back and peered through the screen.

"I'm sorry you had to do that." Elke stood in Shaday's arms, her back against the wall, and tucked a loose strand of jet-black hair behind her ear.

Shaday turned her head and gave Elke's hand a quick kiss. She shrugged. "It wasn't so bad."

Elke frowned. "Do you think she suspects?"

I froze.

Shaday shook her head. "Not really. I spoke with her for a while this afternoon. She asked a lot of questions in roundabout ways, but I don't think she has any idea who it is."

My eyes slid to Iggy's round ones. "She's talking about me," I hissed.

We turned to watch through the screen.

"For now," Elke pouted.

Shaday stroked her thumb under Elke's chin. "I led her to believe it was Muma."

Elke's jaw dropped. "You pinned it on a sixty-year-old servant with a cold?"

Shaday grinned and the light from the lantern at their feet cast her face in deep, shifting shadows. "She doesn't know who Muma is and even if she figures out I was lying, I'll be married and traveling to the Water Kingdom and it'll be easy to avoid her." Shaday smiled at Elke. "And you'll be right there beside me."

I bit my lip and racked my brain. Had we talked about Muma? What did she mean she pinned it on her? I gasped. "She told me her usual henna person was sick," I whispered to Iggy. "Maybe she knows I'm sniffing about trying to solve the murder. Remember, Urs cast a spell that would make any intruder violently ill. Maybe that was her way of getting me to look into Muma, her poor servant."

"Does that mean...". Iggy's eyes grew even wider. "That they killed Elke's father, Bernhardt?"

"I think so." I barely breathed the words. A jolt of excitement coursed through me. I'd solved the mystery. But maybe more than that, the prospect of stopping the wedding made me nearly giddy.

Iggy and I turned back to the screen. Elke and Shaday stood with their heads close together and spoke in whispers. I edged closer and turned my head to hear better. I pressed my ear up to the screen and bumped it with my shoulder. The screen wobbled and my stomach dropped. I fumbled with my free hand to grab it, but it fell forward before I could and clattered to the floor.

That left me holding Iggy and staring across the wide room to Elke and Shaday on the other side of it. They froze in their embrace for a moment, then jumped apart. Elke pressed her hands to her heaving chest and Shaday blinked.

"Imogen?"

"Uhhhh...."

"I hope you're not counting on your legendary way with words to get us out of this," Iggy hissed.

"Oh hi." I waved my fingers at them. "Oh wow, I didn't see you there."

"Sea snakes," Iggy muttered.

My chest flushed hot and I gulped as I edged backward towards the rug. Maybe if I ran I could lose them. I frowned as I remembered Shaday's acrobatics. That was unlikely.

"Were you watching through the screen?" Shaday's eyes flashed. She huffed and turned to Elke. "I forgot that was there. This ridiculous palace and its secret rooms."

"What screen? Oh! Oh, that screen." I gestured lamely to the floor where it lay.

Elke let out a shaky breath and Shaday lifted her henna-covered palms. The same ones that were criss-crossed in scars and burns—strong hands. She stepped toward me. "You're not going to say anything, are you?"

Iggy started screaming and I yanked the shutter on his lamp shut to muffle him. A line formed between Shaday's brows.

"What? Psh." I gave a shrill chuckle and stumbled backward, feeling blindly for the hanging rug and the way out. "No, nope, I won't say anything, please don't kill me."

Shaday straightened. She blinked. She and Elke exchanged puzzled looks. "What?"

I hunched my shoulders up to my ears and squeezed my eyes shut. "I said please don't kill me." Iggy continued to scream.

Deep belly laughter made me peel an eye open. Shaday had folded over, her hands on her stomach, shaking with laughter. Even Elke chuckled. "Kill you? Seriously?"

I cleared my throat, torn between bolting and feeling foolish. "Like you killed Bernhardt?"

Elke's eyes widened. "What are you talking about?"

My eyes darted back and forth from Shaday to Elke and back to Shaday. I winced. "You didn't kill him?"

Elke pressed a hand to her chest. "My father? No!" She scoffed and looked horrified at the suggestion. Shaday straightened and shook her head. "That's ludicrous."

I planted my free hand on my hip. "You guys were just talking about pinning it on Muma, *you* can clearly fight, and Elke, you're trained in hand-to-hand combat. I mean, you're meeting here in secret. It looks pretty suspicious."

Elke folded her arms across her ample chest and cocked one hip. "You're the one hiding behind a screen to watch us meet in secret, which is worse?"

I nodded. "Point taken."

Shaday chuckled. "Come on, Imogen, really? I was talking about a conversation I had this afternoon with this reporter, Madeline L'Orange. She was trying to find out if I knew about Hank's lover. I kept trying to play it down as a ridiculous idea, but she apparently had some believable intel."

I scratched the back of my neck. "That might have been me."

Shaday lifted her dark brows. "Ah. So you're telling your own secrets. Well, maybe I shouldn't have tried to help you then. I pretended to be upset by the idea, saying I'd heard rumors about him and a servant named Muma—that was me pinning it on her." Shaday grinned. "I can't wait for her to try to interrogate Muma."

Elke smirked. "Heaven help her."

I gulped and turned to the blonde young woman. "You didn't want your father to die?"

Elke shrugged. "We weren't close. I'd barely seen him in years, but he left me alone, let me do as I liked. It has always been this way, since my mother died when I was very young. It wasn't that we had a bad relationship, it just wasn't much of one at all." She smiled at Shaday and took her hand. "When I came with him to the Fire Kingdom, years ago, when he trained the men in fighting, I fell in love, and he let me stay without question." She shrugged at me. "I had no reason to want him dead. I disagreed with just about everything he stood for, but he didn't deserve to die like that."

I frowned. "Then why all the secrecy with you training Shaday? Why did you want me to hide your scars and cuts and burns?" I held up my hands.

"First of all." She tilted her head against Elke's. "Our relationship would not be accepted in the Fire Kingdom at large, but especially not by my family. I'm marrying Hank, remember, tomorrow?" She lifted a slim shoulder. "But even if I weren't engaged to another, my mother always wanted a perfect princess and this…" She gestured between her and Elke. "Doesn't jive with her idea of ladylike. We've been careful to keep it a secret—only Muma knows."

I winced. "Guessing your mother wouldn't be a big fan of

the fire-fighting either, then?"

Shaday grinned. "You saw?"

"Yeah, you're amazing."

She grinned wider. "And it looked like fighting to you?"

I shrugged. "I've never seen anything like it." Elke and Shaday exchanged grins. "It was like a mix between kung fu and dancing."

Shaday clapped Elke on the shoulder. "You've never seen anything like it because we made it up." She waved me closer.

I unshuttered Iggy's lantern and muttered, "What do you think?"

He half lowered his lids. "If she wanted you dead, she'd have killed you by now."

I moved past a stack of dining chairs covered in a beige cloth and across the empty expanse of the room. "Just me, huh?"

"I'm too cute to kill." Iggy cackled.

"Right."

When I got close, Shaday pointed at the smoldering veil still on the floor where she'd dropped it. "Elke's a brilliant inventor. She created a new type of fabric that holds enchanted oil for longer. The women of the Fire Kingdom are trained from little girls to dance with fire. We do so by covering our hands and arms and anywhere that might contact the flame with enchanted oil that allows us to handle the fire for longer periods of time, but typically only about twenty to thirty seconds before we have to recoat."

Elke nodded. "At performances, there are always barrels or bowls of the oil placed around the stage or dance floor for the dancers."

I grimaced. "Seems a little dangerous."

"It is, just a little though. The flames we typically dance

with are small and manageable." Shaday bit her lip. "And we
do veil dances—they're just not typically on fire."

I chuckled. "Who knew you were such a daredevil?"

She sighed. "I have a lot of secrets. I've always loved
fighting. When I was little, I convinced the guards to train
me along with my younger brothers. My parents allowed it
until I hit puberty. Didn't matter that I was better than boys
years older than me." She shook her head. "My mother
wanted to raise a typical princess. I suppose I've disap-
pointed her in every way possible."

I frowned. "That can't be true."

Shaday's eyes dropped to her booted feet. "She would be
if she knew who I really am. Anyway, when I was twelve she
pulled me out of fighting and doubled down on the dance
lessons. I hated them. I talked back to my instructor,
skipped lessons, messed up group dances on purpose."

"She was a brat," Elke chimed in.

"True." Shaday grinned at her and I marveled. I still
couldn't get over a smiling, fighting, dancing Shaday. "But I
came around. My instructor had patience with me. She
taught me poise, reserve, grace. She showed me how dance
was a way to express myself."

"And then I showed up." Elke elbowed the princess. "My
father had never minded me learning the technique he and
Urs developed, they encouraged it even. I often helped them
demonstrate the moves for their pupils. I think Shaday fell
for me the day I flipped her on her back and pinned her."

Shaday rolled her eyes. "The next time we grappled, I
did better."

"Because I taught you."

Shaday shook her head at me. "I don't know why I put
up with her."

Elke fluffed her thick, wavy blonde hair and batted her

lashes. "I do."

"Anyway, long story short, we've been together since then—inseparable. We've meshed Elke's fighting with my dancing to create a new style that's a little bit of both. And combined with Elke's inventions, I'm able to handle the fire for longer and in different ways."

"That's incredible, truly. I've never seen anyone move the way you do." I looked between the two of them. "So what's next for this style. Are you going to teach others?"

Shaday's face fell. "Women have a lot of limitations here that they don't in other kingdoms."

Elke rolled her eyes. "Believe me. They all have limitations."

"Yes, but you're allowed to learn martial arts where you're from." Shaday stared at her girlfriend and Elke nodded in agreement. The princess turned back to me and Iggy. "Here, even though I'm the eldest, I can't rule, can't be queen of my own people, because I'm a woman. I can't openly be with the person I love...."

I sighed. "I feel you there."

"I have to marry someone else instead. My whole life is being used as a political tool, as if my only worth is as a bargaining chip." She huffed. "I deserve better. The people of Calloon deserve better."

"I'm sorry." I shook my head. "Honestly. It's not fair. And for what it's worth, I think you'd make a kick-ass queen."

Elke grinned. "Yeah, she would."

Shaday sighed. "Thank you both."

"I agree," Iggy chimed in.

Shaday lifted a brow. "And thank you, Iggy." She raised her decorated palms. "So, do you believe that we didn't kill Elke's father?"

Heat burned up my neck and I bit my lip. "Yeah... I'm

really sorry about that. I think, I think I just let my imagination get the best of me. You've never been anything but kind and thoughtful. I'm sorry I thought that of you, even for a moment."

Shaday quirked her lips to the side. "It's all right. I know you're having a hard time right now, too." She squeezed my hand, her own rough and hard. "We ladies have to stick together." She nodded at Elke. "I'm going to go do my cooldown." She moved away and plopped down on the tiled floor to stretch.

Elke walked up to me.

"I'm sorry, Elke. I didn't think through how harsh that accusation sounded. I'm sorry for the loss of your father."

She pressed her full lips together. "Like Shaday said, I think we're all going through a lot right now." She gave me a sad smile. "Guess we have a lot more in common than I would have guessed. We both have to watch the people we love marry someone else tomorrow."

My chest grew tight. I gulped and tried to shake it off.

"Shaday thought it might be good for us to talk. She thought we might hit it off as friends and the sky knows, I need someone to talk to about this right now. Someone who understands."

I shrugged, then cleared my throat. I really didn't want to talk about this at all, especially with someone I hardly knew. "Elke. I'm sorry you're having a hard time, and I'm sure Shaday's right, that we could be great friends, but I—I'm really doing all right. Not great, but I'm hanging in there."

She blinked at me with her soft brown eyes. "Really?" She sighed. "I'm having daily meltdowns. I cried into my porridge this morning—turned it salty."

I clicked my tongue and rubbed her shoulder. "I'm so sorry." I shook my head. "I'm just really tired tonight. But maybe we can talk more tomorrow?" Maybe after it was all done and over with, that pit in my stomach would disappear and I could talk about it without my throat getting tight. "I'm sorry. We'll talk tomorrow, but I should get to bed."

"Oh. All right." Elke blinked at me and my stomach tightened with the realization that I'd hurt her feelings a little. I waved at Shaday and carried Iggy out through the secret doorway behind the hanging rug and down the hallway.

"That was rude."

I bit my lip and held back tears. "Not now, Iggy, okay? I just couldn't talk to her right now."

I stormed forward, barely aware of where I was headed. I rounded a corner, my eyes on the ground and my head whirling with thoughts. "Why does everyone insist on trying to make me talk about it when I keep telling them I don't want to?" I grumbled.

"Ooh." Iggy cleared his throat. "Imogen."

I sighed. "I just told you, I don't want to—"

"Imogen?"

I stopped dead and slowly raised my eyes. Hank stood directly in front of me. He sighed, and I noticed how tired he looked. Dark bags drooped below his eyes and he looked paler than usual. He stepped up to me and threw his strong arms around me in a tight hug. I took a deep breath and noted he smelled of cardamom today. He liked to pop into the bakery, and he always picked up the scent of spices and sugar and baking bread. In other words, he smelled delicious. My stomach turned with longing and sadness and I pulled out of the hug. He blinked at me.

"Imogen, I've been looking all over for you." His thick brows pulled together. "For the last two days, actually."

My heart rate picked up.

"I need to talk to you."

15

ISLAND GETAWAY

I sighed and shrugged. Iggy's lantern dangled from my hand. I really, *really* didn't want to talk about this. "Like I've been saying, I'm *fine*."

Hank stepped closer and I dropped my eyes to his broad chest. He wore his uniform again, with that broad blue sash across his white coat. The light of the nearest wall sconce danced off it. "Well, I'm not." His deep voice came out hoarse and I looked up into his bloodshot eyes.

He shoved a hand through his dark hair, roughly pulling it back. "I miss you. For months we've been spending every minute together and now I can't even get you to talk to me."

I swallowed against the tight lump in my throat and looked away. It was true. Since Bruma, even before that, we'd been practically inseparable. Even when I was working, he snuck down to the bakery and worked alongside us at least once a day. And at night we went on dates in the royal library or gardens or joined our friends for a pint at the Rusted Wreck in town. It'd been wonderful... and now it felt like it was all over.

Hank sighed and gripped my shoulders. "You're *still* not talking to me. Is this what it's going to be like?"

I lifted my eyes to his and willed them wider to hold in the tears that were brimming almost to overflow.

"Because I can't do this." He shook his head, his face pinched with pain. I hated to see him like this. "I can't go back to the way I was living before I met you. I can't lose you."

I swallowed. It hurt. I licked my lips as a tear escaped and trailed down my cheek. I swiped it away. "I don't like this any more than you do. Believe me." I pressed my lips into a tight line and shrugged. "But this is how it is, right? I knew that from the beginning."

Hank squeezed my arms and searched my face. "I should've told you this earlier, but I didn't want you to feel responsible or guilty if I—if I decided to call off the wedding."

My brows jumped and chills spread over me. "Are you thinking of doing that?" I asked it carefully, slowly, trying not to let myself hope or to show him how much I'd hoped for him to do that. I hadn't even realized how much I'd wanted it until this moment.

"Imogen." He shook his head, his blue eyes wet and sparkling in the firelight. "I've thought about it since we almost kissed in the baking tent—every day, I've thought about it. I would've have called it off by now, but I'm beholden to my father's line of magic. All of my brothers are, too. It's been that way for generations. My magic is tied to Bijou Mer and to the ruler of it, my father. If I called off this wedding—" Hank let out a dry, humorless chuckle. "He'd be beyond furious. I'm not high in my father's esteem anyway. I've always been the black sheep of the family. He hates that I enjoy baking, hates that I'm a swallow and different. I catch him watching me sometimes from across the room or at a feast—he's always glaring at me." Hank shook himself. "It doesn't matter, except that I have no doubt he would disown me and that would mean losing my powers, my magic." His chest heaved. "I should've told you earlier, but I wanted you to feel comfortable expressing what you wanted, even if that meant asking me to call off the engagement. I kept waiting for you to. And when you didn't, I tried to talk to you about it, but you've been avoiding me."

My eyes slid to the side. "I've been busy."

"I heard you got banned from the bakery."

"So what if I did?" My eyes flashed.

"I just mean, it's clear you're upset. I wish you'd tell me how you feel," Hank pleaded with me. His brows lifted and his breath came in short pants.

Tears ran down my cheeks. "I love you, okay? And this is horrible." The dam had broken. The tears poured now and my words came out between sobs. "Francis told me in Wee Ferngroveshire about your father's power over you. I already knew; that's why I didn't say anything. I couldn't ask that of you."

He stepped closer. "Yes, you could."

I shook my head, my vision blurred by my tears. "No, I couldn't. Your magic is a part of who you are. So is being a prince. I couldn't ask you to give up who you are. Even if I really, really want to." I hung my head and my shoulders shook. "This is why I didn't want to talk about this, because I can't." I covered my eyes with one hand and wept. My chest ached and I felt like there was no end to the tears. It's why I'd tried to avoid them in the first place. Now that I'd started, I didn't know if I could ever stop crying.

Hank pulled me into another hug and I sagged against

him. My whole body shook with my sobs as he stroked my back and held me tight. This sucked.

After a while, I stopped, and my breathing settled down with the occasional shuddering gulp. I pulled back and looked Hank in the face. His nose and eyes were red and I wiped a tear from his cheek with my fingertip.

I sighed. "Get married. We'll figure something out. I just don't think we're going to figure it out tonight."

Hank clasped my hand in his own and held it to his face. "If you can't make this situation work, then it won't work for me, either."

I sniffed but gave a tight nod. I wiped my snotty face on my shoulder. "We'll make it work. But I've got to get some sleep. You do, too. Big day tomorrow."

Hank kissed my forehead and whispered, "I love you." I breathed in the sweet, spicy smell of him one more time and then we parted ways. I walked away, willing my steps to be slow, and didn't look back. As soon as I'd rounded the corner I broke into a run.

"Whoa!" Iggy, still in the lantern in my hand, cried out. "You okay?"

I couldn't answer. I'd managed to stifle my sobs for long enough to get out of that hallway, but I couldn't hold them in anymore. I let out a deep moan and stumbled down dark hallway after hallway.

"Imogen? Where are we going?"

I ignored Iggy and cursed the mazelike palace. I just had to get out of it. I felt like I was suffocating. Finally, I found the empty bakery, dark except for the low glow from the snoozing oven fires. I dashed out the back door and into the cool night air of the alleyway. My throat burned with my rasping breaths and I leaned against the plaster wall behind me. I set Iggy carefully on the gravelly ground at my feet and buried my face in my trembling hands.

"Imogen?" Iggy's fire warmed my ankles as he peeked out of the lantern. "What can I do? You're not okay."

I shook my head. "Nothing. You can't do anything, no one can. It's just—" I sobbed. "It's just the way it is."

Iggy let me cry for a while, then suddenly the little flame spoke up. "Imogen? Hey, Imogen!"

I sniffed. "Whad?" My voice came out deep and stuffed up.

"Hey. Look over there."

I glanced down at Iggy. He leaned halfway out of his lantern, pointing with an orange arm of flame. I followed his gaze to a nearby archway made of blue plaster that had crumbled away in spots and exposed the tan brick underneath. Two golden eyes glowed from the shadows. I froze. Then, keeping my eyes on the shadows, I slowly reached to my right, feeling around for the doorknob back into the bakery. I breathed out a little sigh of relief when my hand closed around the knob, but the feeling was short-lived. I turned the knob and it stuck. I jiggled it and tugged.

"The door's locked, Iggy." I bit my lip.

"Not good...." Iggy flashed brighter.

A large, shaggy black dog that looked half wolf stepped forward from the shadows, its eyes glowing gold.

"Oh, hey doggy." I gave a weak smile.

"Sea snakes!" Iggy huffed. "You're gonna have to do better than that."

"Like what?" I snatched Iggy up off the ground and hugged the lantern to me, my back pressed against the wall.

"Like magic! You're a witch, remember?"

My chest heaved. "Right, right... I can't think of any spells!"

The dog walked straight at us, slow and steady, and suddenly, in the blink of an eye, where the dog had been, Horace stood.

I sagged with relief. "Oh, thank goodness, I thought—"

Iggy cut me off with an ear-splitting scream. My eyes widened. He kept screaming. Some dogs nearby started barking.

"Iggy, sh! You're going to wake everyone up."

"Good!" He threw his head back and opened his round mouth as wide as it went and screamed some more.

"Iggy!" Panicked, I shut the shutter on the lantern, which muted him somewhat. I looked up at Horace. "I'm sorry. I'm sure he'll stop soon... ish."

Iggy stopped on a dime and I cautiously slid the shutter back open. He frowned. "Did you just apologize to him?" He blinked up at me.

My stomach dropped. Oh right. I hadn't told him about Horace. I took a deep breath and spoke slowly. "Iggy. I didn't tell you *everything* I did yesterday."

His jaw hung open and his eyes widened. "What are you saying?"

I let out a heavy breath. "I met up with Horace."

"You met up with Horace?!"

"You have to stop screaming," I hissed.

He glared at me.

"He is my brother, you know, I'm allowed to be curious about him, to want to get to know him."

"He's a wanted criminal." Iggy looked at me like I was crazy.

I sighed. "Yes. But he's also the one who saved me as a child and my only relative. He's not going to hurt me, or you." I looked up at Horace, suddenly less sure. "Right?"

"Correct." Horace stared at me with his half-lowered lids. "Can I approach, or will your pet lose its mind again?"

Iggy's jaw dropped and he huffed with indignation. He turned to address Horace. "First of all, I am *not* her pet. And secondly, I will scream whenever I feel threatened by international terrorists who can apparently turn into dogs." Iggy rounded on me. "Did you know he can turn into a dog?"

My lips quirked to the side. "I just found out. Apparently, I can too."

Iggy's eyes widened. "You think you know a person."

I rolled my eyes. "Oh, hush. You know me." I lifted Iggy up. "Horace, Iggy. Iggy, Horace."

Iggy folded his flame arms and Horace lifted one lazy brow.

"Right. Warm and fuzzies all around." I sighed.

Horace nodded at Iggy. "I'm sorry to intrude." He looked at me and something besides his usual mask of boredom flashed across his eyes. "But you seemed to be in distress."

I chuckled and it ended as a sob. "You could say that."

"Are you hurt?" Horace stepped closer and Iggy started growling. I shot him a look and he stopped.

I shook my head. "No. I mean, yes, emotionally, not physically." I dipped my chin and pulled a hand through my bangs. "It just—I think it just really hit me, for the first time, that this wedding is really happening. I think a part of me, a big part, thought that Hank would back out or, more recently, that Shaday would turn out to have killed Bernhardt and the wedding would be called off, or something would stop it."

I swallowed, trying to push down that lump in my throat. Tears welled up in my eyes all over again. "But—but he's not going to, and Shaday's not the killer. In fact, she's even more wonderful than I thought, and I don't know what to do. I think Hank half wanted me to ask him to end it with Shaday, but that would mean losing his powers and everything—his family. I can't possibly want that or expect that —" I groaned and folded over, the sobs returning. "But I still do! I still want that, if I'm honest, and I feel terrible for it!" I couldn't speak, but Horace and Iggy let me cry.

Tears fell from my eyes to the sandy ground below. The blurry tips of Horace's shoes appeared on the ground in front of me and then he wrapped his arms around me in a hug. It was light and tentative at first, but I rested my head against him and his arms tightened around me.

"Look at you," I gulped out between tears. "Being all brotherly."

A deep chuckle rumbled in Horace's throat.

"Hurt her, and I'll burn you where you stand," Iggy hissed, still dangling from my hand.

Horace ignored him and spoke in his deep, laconic voice. "Come with me."

I stiffened.

"For as long as you like. I'll show you around the Badlands, it's beautiful."

I sniffed. "Your home?"

He cleared his throat. "I have no home."

"Imogen...." Iggy's voice rose at the end, a warning.

"You need to get away from here, it's a toxic situation, toxic people—look what they're doing to you with their elitist rules of who can marry who, the king's need to control everything, even his own children. You need to get away from it all."

It was tempting. An island, a break, a chance to connect with my brother. But I imagined telling Maple and my stomach twisted. I wasn't sure I was ready to leave her and all my friends behind.

"I—I have to think about it." I leaned back and looked up at his shadowed eyes.

He blinked. "I'm leaving tomorrow, during the wedding. Meet me at the base of the volcano if you decide to join me."

The wedding. I didn't think I could bear it. And yet, leaving my friends to join Horace, even for a short time...I wasn't sure if they'd accept that decision.

I sniffed. "Thank you, for the offer. I really will think about it."

"Do."

Horace backed away and disappeared into the shadows.

Iggy rounded on me. "You can't be seriously considering this." When I didn't answer, he gasped. "Imogen!"

"This is killing me, Iggy. Working Hank's wedding, knowing nothing is ever going to be the same again." I shook my head. "I think I just need a break."

"A break is going rainbow sliding in the Air Kingdom. What you're talking about is practically treason!"

I rolled my eyes. "You're exaggerating." I swallowed. "And also, is rainbow sliding a real thing? Because that sounds amazing."

I started off with him around the side of the palace. Since the bakery door was locked, we'd probably have to go all the way around and head in the front entrance.

"You're missing the point. I'm worried about you. People aren't going to understand why you're consorting with the leader of the Badlands Army."

I licked my lips. "I know, some won't. Maybe no one will understand. But he's my brother and I feel safe with him. I need to understand him and know him better. And going with him to the Badlands would be a way to do that and give myself some time to accept Hank and Shaday being married. Because I don't know if I can go back to Bijou Mer next week and wake up in the morning to bake them their favorite muffins for breakfast in bed." The thought made me feel more depressed than I could express.

"Hmph. Well, I'll tell you that *I* don't understand why you have to go with Horace." Iggy sniffed. "But I'm still going with you if you do."

"What?" I held the lantern up to my face.

Iggy glared. "I'm not letting you walk into monster island all alone with the world's most wanted criminal."

My lip trembled. "Iggy...."

"Nuh-uh." He shook his head. "No more tears, you're cried out for tonight. Any more and you're going to shrivel up from dehydration and they'll just find your wrinkled skin tomorrow morning all stiff like beef jerky."

I chuckled. "Quite the imagery, thank you for that." I sighed. "Thank you, Iggy. I don't know if I'll go with him or not, but I appreciate you having my back, no matter what."

"You bet I do. Your shriveled, dehydrated jerky back."

16

LOVE TRIANGLE

I t was the next afternoon, the day of the wedding, and we had nearly finished with the cake. My friends and I worked alongside the Fire Kingdom bakers to assemble the seven-tiered giant beauty. A few of their bakers and Yann worked a spell that lowered the temperature in the bakery to keep the buttercream frosting from melting.

I even kept Iggy in his lantern on the tiled countertop, away from our workstation, to keep the air near the cakes cool. No fires were needed anymore. All the cakes had already been baked and frosted.

And now came the assembly and final decorations. I bit my nail. I always found this the most nerve-wracking part.

Maple and Wool directed Annie and a baker from Fire as they spelled the cakes together, the biggest circle on bottom, then the next biggest and next, until they finally placed the smallest tier, only as big around as a salad plate, on top. We all let out a collective sigh of relief and I joined the others in clapping my hands.

Wiley squeezed Annie's shoulder. "Well done, didn't know you still had the hand-eye coordination at your age."

She glared and yanked the kitchen towel off of her shoulder and snapped it at him. He jumped away, but it got his thigh.

"Ow!"

Annie chuckled.

Next, I helped a few other bakers pipe gold beads between the seams of the cake tiers, while others followed behind us, magically dusted the frosting with shimmering gold dust that sparkled and glowed. Maple trailed behind me, gilding the beads I made.

She lowered her voice. "I'm dying here."

I lifted my brows, then rolled my eyes. "Geez. I'm so sorry, I forgot to ask." I'd been pretty busy with wallowing in self-pity since last night, and my stomach churned as my decision about joining Horace loomed closer. I glanced at the big clock on the wall, the second hand ticking away. The wedding started in just over an hour. I shook myself and glanced at Maple. "Tell me how your date went?"

She gave me shy smile. "It was perfect. We went to this charming place for dinner, they treated him like family." She shook her head. "I swear, everyone loves him. The food was delicious. I had lamb with rice pilaf and this creamy hummus—"

I grinned. "Stop, you're making my stomach growl."

She shook her head and a blonde tendril fell out of her ponytail. "Then we went to the bakery he mentioned and they gave us a private lesson in making baklava by candlelight."

"Wow. Sounds romantic."

She nodded. "It was. So romantic. And he was such a gentleman, and funny and easy to talk to." She shook her head and her face fell. "He's perfect."

I frowned and smiled, at the same time. "So... what's the problem?"

She huffed, then dropped her voice when a few eyes slid our way. "That's the problem. He's absolutely perfect and yet I can't stop thinking about Wiley who, in comparison—"

"Looks like a half-formed man-child?"

She giggled, but nodded. "What is wrong with me?"

I grinned. "You're in love. It makes us all idiots."

She paled. "You think?" She pressed her eyes closed and whimpered. "Oh no. You're right. I've been trying to fight it but—hmph!" She balled her small hands into fists. "I love Wiley." Her shoulders slumped. "I'm doomed."

I laughed. "That's a bit of an exaggeration, don't you think?" I nudged her shoulder. "Tell him how you feel."

She peered around the side of the cake. Wiley and Wool stood a few feet away on the other side of the table where they worked together to place the beautiful, enchanted frosting flowers on top of the cake. They were so tall, they didn't need to stand on stools like the rest of us would have.

"He's not into me anymore."

I scoffed. "Please."

"He isn't." She shook her head. "He told me to go out with Wool. I think he's more into *him* now than he was ever into me."

I peered around the other side of the cake and caught Wiley leaning back with his arms wrapped around Wool's middle, steadying him as Wool rose on tiptoe to place the last flowers on top. "Okay. You may have a point there." We finished the beaded seam and stepped back. All the other bakers did the same within a few moments, and we marveled at our creation. With so many of us working together, it'd gone smoother and faster than I would have imagined. Tiers of midnight blue cakes dotted and laced with glowing gold frosting stood before us. Edible flowers, magically blooming and blowing in an imaginary breeze tumbled from the top down the sides.

Wiley held up a few bottles of champagne. "I snagged these from the bar—figured we should celebrate."

We broke into cheers, and soon everyone had a cup or mug of champagne and we stood around, chatting and celebrating our accomplishment before hundreds of hungry guests devoured it.

Annie sighed. "I just wish they could last longer." She took a gulp of champagne and batted her eyes at the cake. "It's just so lovely."

I threw an arm over her shoulders and gave her a hug. "It is." I lifted my coffee mug and clinked it against her blown-glass cup. I headed toward Wool to thank him for being such a lovely host, when Maple beat me to the punch. She swayed slightly. Uh-oh. I'd forgotten what a lightweight she was with alcohol, even champagne.

"I had a great time on our date last night." She put a hand on Wool's arm. "Thank you, again." Her eyes slid to Wiley.

He flushed a little redder at the collar, but kept a grin on his face.

Maple turned to face Wiley, straight on. "So glad you encouraged me to go." She balled her hands and Wool frowned as he watched the exchange.

Wiley's chest puffed up. "I'm so, so glad that I did, too."

Maple stepped closer, Wool completely forgotten. Gradually the other bakers had quieted as they noticed the situation. Maple held her arms stiff at her sides. "This could have been awkward. So glad it isn't."

"Me, too," Wiley ground out through gritted teeth. "You have no idea how relieved I feel."

Maple's nostrils flared and her cheeks flushed bright pink. "Good. Then you won't feel uncomfortable if I give him a kiss to thank him?"

My eyes slid to K'ree's round ones. She pulled her mouth wide into a grimace.

"What is happening?" I mouthed.

When Wiley didn't answer, Maple spun on her heel and marched a couple quick steps up to Wool, who threw his huge hands up in surrender. She puckered her lips and rose up to plant a kiss on his cheek.

Wiley let out a shrill whine from between his teeth as he held his face in a manic smile that looked more like a monkey baring its teeth. "It's all good." The mug in his hand exploded, and ceramic shards clanked to the tile floor along with what remained of his champagne. I knew that move— I'd exploded a glass just two nights ago at Hank's engagement feast. My stomach tightened as I glanced at the clock. Only forty-five minutes to go until the ceremony.

Maple whirled around on Wiley, leaving Wool shaken. "What in the waves? You just said—"

Wiley stepped forward, his chest jutting out and his jaw set. "I know what I said." His chest heaved and a thick vein bulged in his red neck. "I'm trying to control my emotions to be better for you, and me. But a lot for you!"

Iggy gave a slow clap behind me. "And you're doing a great job."

Wool lifted a long finger. "If I may?" Wiley and Maple's wild eyes swung to him and he winced. "We've been talking about being more mindful, Wiley, and that's just being aware of your emotions, not suppressing them or judging them." He grimaced. "And perhaps finding healthier ways to express them."

I shook my head. "He is perfect."

K'ree let out a dreamy sigh.

Maple turned back to Wiley and folded her arms. "So, then. Express away."

"I love you!" Wiley practically shouted.

A collective gasp rose up from among us bakers. Annie pressed both hands to her mouth.

Wiley's chest heaved as he moved up to Maple and looked down at her. "I love you. And it's driving me crazy that you went out with Wool, but who wouldn't want him? I mean, look at him!" Wiley threw an arm toward Wool and the women in the room nodded. Wiley's pinched face looked crushed. "And on top of all that charm and perfect hair, he's wise and funny and confident and I'm just—"

Maple closed the gap between them, grabbed his face, pulled it down to hers and kissed him. My jaw dropped in shock and the bakery went silent. Goose bumps crept up my arms and tears of happiness for my friend welled in my eyes.

Iggy let out a piercing whistle and broke the silence.

Maple and Wiley laughed, and leaned their foreheads together, still holding each other. Then Maple gasped and spun around.

"Wool, I'm so sorry."

He grinned and held up his hands. "Don't be. You two clearly belong together." He shrugged. "I'm happy to just be friends, with both of you."

I chuckled, wondering if Wool felt like he'd dodged a bullet. Wiley smiled his thanks, then pulled Maple into another kiss, and I clapped along with the other bakers. But as I stared past the wedding cake and watched the beginning of my friends' love story, my stomach sank and cold swept through me. This would be Hank and Shaday soon, very soon. The ticking of the clock's second hand seemed to pound into my brain.

Tick tock. Tick tock.

My breathing came in short gasps and I backed up, slamming into the counter.

"Uh, Imogen... you okay?" Iggy peeked out of his lantern. His eyes widened when he saw me. "Oh goddess. You're gonna do it."

My chest heaved as I struggled to breathe. Was this what a panic attack felt like? I wanted to rip my shirt off. I felt like something was choking me.

"Breathe," Iggy hissed.

"I can't. I can't be here anymore." I struggled to inhale. I'd hesitated last night, worried about leaving my friends. But seeing Maple happy in Wiley's arms, I knew they'd be fine without me. I'd go, just for a little while.

"I'm coming with," Iggy reminded me.

I grabbed his lantern and spun. I dashed out the back door of the bakery without a single person noticing, they were all too busy celebrating the cake and congratulating Wiley and Maple. I'd send her a letter or something—I'd let her and everyone else know I was okay as soon as I could.

But for now, I just had to get to Damavash Volcano in time to meet my brother.

17

RING OF FIRE

"**O**w! Ow! Ow!" I bounced in the leather saddle as my camel galloped its way across the sands. My hips ached from the ride. I had to shift every minute or so to keep from getting burned by Iggy's lantern, which I held in my lap with one arm, while navigating the reins with the other. I was shocked I hadn't fallen off.

I squinted into the bright afternoon sun. A tiny speck stood out at the base of the looming volcano.

"I think I see him."

We'd just passed the camp where we'd had the feast and where Bernhardt had been killed. I prayed that I wasn't too late, and that I'd find Horace waiting for me. I leaned forward and ignored the stinging as the lantern heated up my stomach. I snapped the reins and urged the camel faster. I'd found a Rent-a-Camel stand in the marketplace and the merchant had assured me this was his fastest one. I hoped he was right.

Before us the wide, flat-topped volcano dominated the skyline, with the smaller sandy mountains that helped form the desert valley scattered around its base. As we neared, the figure grew larger and I could make out the outline of a person. It had to be Horace.

"You're sure you want to do this?" Iggy called up to me over the clop of the camel's hooves. The wind whistled in my ears as it blew against us, back toward Calloon.

I shook my head, loose strands of hair whipping me in the eyes. "No! But I need to see where this goes with Horace." My stomach twisted. Because I already knew where it went with Hank. Had his wedding already started? I felt like I might be sick. Was it already over? I shook myself. It didn't matter. I focused on staying atop the camel and guiding it toward the figure up ahead.

When we reached the base of the volcano, Horace stood in his usual all black with his archaeologist's bag of rolled papers, waiting for me. He helped me down from the camel.

I gave a little shrug. "I came."

His face softened. "I wasn't sure you would." He nodded. "But I'm glad." His eyes slid to Iggy. "You're bringing *it*?"

I lifted my index finger. "Him."

"I'm right here, you know." Iggy crossed his fire arms.

Horace sniffed but didn't say anything further about it. He turned toward the volcano and together we tipped our heads back to look toward the summit, which lay out of sight, obscured by a ring of clouds. He slid his half-lidded gaze toward me. "Ready?" He slung his bag across his chest and reached out for my free hand.

I froze. "For what?"

His lips quirked to the side as he jerked his chin toward the summit. "To go to the top."

I shook my head and stepped back. "No. No way. You're joking."

"Do I look like I'm joking?" He gave me a lazy blink.

"Uh, no, never, actually." I gulped and shook my head again. "But you know, I'm not a big hiker." I eyed the loose black rock that was no doubt razor-sharp and sloped steeply to the summit. I spotted no obvious path. "Yeah, no."

He let out a little sigh. "I've hidden a portal mirror in the caldera. It's the way to the Badlands and you're late. We need to get up there immediately." He reached his hand out again for mine. I glanced nervously back at the camel, which had folded its knees under and lain down. I could turn back, head to the palace, pretend I'd never had this crazy scheme. My stomach twisted. Maybe make it in time to see Hank say his vows.

I took a deep breath and let it out in a rush. I grabbed Horace's large, cool hand, and he squeezed mine tightly. "So how do we get up?"

"Hold on tight."

My eyes widened. I had just enough time to squeeze his hand and wrap my fingers tight around the lantern loop before I lurched forward, tugged along by Horace, and found myself halfway up the volcano. I'd left my stomach somewhere behind, and as we rocketed up the nearly vertical slope, gazing at mostly sky and cloud, I found my voice and screamed at the top of my lungs. My legs were a blur underneath me, racing to keep up with Horace. The air grew hotter and hotter and suddenly, we flew over a lip. I lurched upright and stumbled over my own feet towards a churning pit of fire and black crust.

I circled my arms, threw my weight back and dug my heels in as I skidded toward the edge. A sharp yank on my left shoulder brought me up short. I recoiled and fell against Horace, who'd pulled me back, the lantern swinging wildly in my right hand.

"Hurggh." Iggy vomited a cloud of ash.

My chest heaved as Horace steadied me and pushed me upright. "I... hate... the speed spell."

Horace's nostrils flared and he cast a mildly disgusted glance at Iggy and his ash vomit. As Horace walked closer to the edge of swirling orange lava, I looked around and took in where we were. Below us, the caldera formed a bowl of churning black crust, split by cracks of orange fire that spurted liquid flame now and then. I tucked my face into the crook of my elbow and coughed. A haze of gases rose from the circular pit before me. Even if Iggy hadn't lost his lunch from motion sickness, the overwhelming odor of sulfur probably would have done the trick.

"The Fire Kingdom food is really not agreeing with you, huh?" Iggy chirped.

I frowned... then rolled my eyes. "Clever." Then, because I couldn't help myself, "Besides, whoever smelt it dealt it."

I wiped my wet forehead on my shoulder, then dabbed at my upper lip. I took a step and looked down in horror. As if I'd stepped in a giant piece of gum, strands of rubber stretched from the rock to the bottom of my sneaker. My jaw dropped. My shoes were melting. It was so hot, my shoes were melting. I dashed up to my brother and shook his arm.

"How is this possible? Why aren't we spontaneously combusting?" I glanced at the swirling gases above the pit of fire. "Is it safe to breath this stuff?" My throat and chest stung.

He smirked. "I'm pulling energy from the volcano to keep the air around us cool." He glanced back at the trail of rubber behind me. "Without the spell, we wouldn't have lasted a moment."

I gulped. "Well, you certainly picked a good hiding spot for the portal mirror."

He pointed to a gleaming rectangle that sat on an

outcropping of rock just barely above the edge of the lava. A narrow ledge circled the caldera down to it. My jaw dropped. "We have to go down there to go through?"

He nodded.

"Uh—isn't putting it there a bit of overkill?"

His eyes flashed. They reflected the churning orange lava and black rock, and I shrunk back a little. "There's a reason." He checked his wristwatch. "And you'll see why in just a moment. Back in the Badlands, an associate is going to open the portal for a very limited amount of time. Enough time for someone to come out, and for *someones*"—he gestured between us—"to enter. However, if we're not through the portal by five after, my associate has instructions to destroy the mirror, lest an enemy use it."

I frowned. "That doesn't give us much time. It's nearly four now, right?" I peeked at his watch. The wedding must be just about to start. "And what did you mean by someone coming out?"

"That's a great question, Imogen." Iggy said in a high, stressed voice. "One I don't have a great feeling about."

At that moment a bright green flash turned the portal mirror into a swirling vortex of glowing light. A figure gradually grew larger and larger in the frame until it nearly blotted out the shining green light entirely. A serpent, a dinosaur-sized snake, magically squeezed through the impossibly small opening. Its pointed head came first, black as the volcanic rock around us, and then the rest of its huge, dark body slithered out behind. It dove into the caldera and sent up a spray of bright gold lava.

I leapt back and tried to pull Horace with me, but he didn't budge. He turned his head. "Come on. It's time to go."

My eyes widened and I tilted my head toward the pool of lava. "A monster just came through the portal and is right there." I frowned and crinkled my nose at the smell of burning lava. "If it's still alive."

Horace's mouth pulled into a wry grin. "I call him Tar."

"Like, *the* Tar, from that legend they told me about the serpent that lived in this volcano?"

He shrugged. "I'm not sure if it's *the* Tar, but I'm sure many will assume so. And yes, he's very much alive. You see, he feeds on fire. It makes him bigger, stronger. It's why I put the portal mirror here—what better source of fire than this?"

My heart thundered in my chest and my wide eyes stung from the heat, even under the spell's protection. "You mean, you meant for him to come through?" I coughed into my shoulder.

"Yes. And like I said, it's time to go. The portal's closing soon." He stepped down the path and beckoned me to follow.

"Wait, what's going to happen when we leave? Is Tar going to stay up here or—"

The churning lava and dark rock reflected off Horace's eyes in such a way that one glowed orange and the other pitch-black. Goose bumps crawled up my arms as he flashed me a grim smile. "We'll see if anyone is as brave as Damavash was."

I gasped. "Tar's going to attack the town."

Horace let out a short sigh. "Obviously." He beckoned me forward but I stayed rooted to the spot, and not just because my shoes were melting to the rock.

"Horace, why?" My voice trembled. "I can't leave knowing this monster is going to attack Hank and my friends and all the people in the city. We have to stop this. Send it back through!"

My brother's face darkened. "You've seen how corrupt

they are. The golden prince has broken your heart—he should pay for that. You chose me over them, over him."

I balled my fists and tear sprang to my eyes. "Hank doesn't have a choice. He's not a bad person."

Horace sneered. "He's a grown man. Of course he has a choice, but he's choosing to maintain the status quo, to please dear ol' daddy. Who, by the way, deserves to be thrown into this pit, not have his every whim honored. He's choosing his family over you." He practically growled. "I thought you'd chosen family, too."

I let out a sob. "I want to know you, I do, that's why I'm here. But it wasn't a choice of you over them." I threw my arm back toward where I guessed the city lay under the ring of clouds. "They're my friends. I can't just leave them to fight this thing alone." I shook my head. "Especially when you're the one who set it on them."

"This is what they deserve!" Horace bellowed.

"No, it's not!" I screamed back.

We glared at each other, chests heaving, and I suddenly realized that I stood atop a volcano filled with a writhing fire monster that was sending up bigger and bigger sprays of lava as it swam, with the kingdoms' most wanted criminal, who was no longer feeling so warm and fuzzy toward me.

"I'm your family, Imogen." His voice came out hoarse, and he beat a fist to his chest. "Me." His lips curled back. "You're going to choose them, people you barely know, over me? Your brother?"

I thought of Hank and Maple and Sam and all the others. I shook my head as tears fell from my eyes and evaporated on my cheeks. "You can't ask me to choose."

For just a moment, a look of deep hurt crossed his face. And then it was gone, replaced by his usual bored expression. "You just did." He shifted his bag of papers and started down the path. My chest heaved as I watched him go. More tears fell. He turned back. "As soon as I go through here," he shouted up to me as he pointed at the swirling green vortex, "that protective spell will end. I suggest you be ready."

I choked on panic.

"One," Horace shouted.

"Find a source," Iggy reminded me.

I closed my eyes and searched. The enormous bowl of liquid fire jumped out at me.

"Two!"

"Pull from it and make us a bubble," Iggy shouted.

I squeezed my eyes shut and opened myself to a flood of magic energy.

"Three!"

A green flash made me flick my eyes open. Horace stepped through the portal and just as the protective spell he'd cast burst, I threw my own around Iggy and me. My chest caught. I'd saved us from burning up... though I wasn't sure how that would've affected Iggy.

"Oh goddess." My flame panted. "Good job, Imogen."

I grinned. "Wow, actual sincerity."

"Don't get used to it."

The glass of the portal mirror shattered and I jumped. Horace wasn't kidding about breaking the connection.

"We're trapped up here." I looked around and roughly wiped my face on my shoulder again. The world spun a little. "I can't last in this heat for too long."

"Well, if you're lucky the fire monster will get you first."

"So positive."

He shrugged. "I'm a caldera-half-full kinda guy."

"Do you see a path down or anything?" I moved to the mountain edge and peered over the side. My already light head spun even more and I stepped back. "I'm going to be sick."

"It's the only way." Iggy sighed. "Come on. You're going to have to use the speed spell and hope it's more of a controlled fall than anything."

I shook my head. "Oh no. I can't. Going down's even worse than up."

Behind us, a deep roar sounded, low and rumbling at first. Then it rose, louder and higher until it ended in a shrill shriek, like an angry child's.

I shuddered as goose bumps prickled my arms. "I'm so creeped out."

I looked back. A clawed hand, as big as a car, thumped down on the lip of the caldera, crushing large, sharp rocks beneath it.

"Oh, I see it has legs now." Iggy's voice came out shrill.

The snake-like head appeared next. Its round eyes glowed orange, shining against its black, charred skin. It looked as if the lava had come alive, the black-plated skin like the crust that formed over the lava, crisscrossed with streaks of fiery orange. It tilted its head to the sky and screamed again as fire and black smoke erupted from its sharp-toothed mouth. I scrambled away, right up to the cliff's edge, to get as much distance between us and it as possible. The bubble of protection around us shimmered and shrank, faltering under the heat as I grew weaker and woozier.

"Imogen, now or never!" Iggy yelled.

Tar threw himself up over the lip, then moved in a wriggling, flopping way toward us.

I used every ounce of willpower I possessed to turn myself around, grip Iggy's lantern tight, and then pull magic from the energy of the lava. I lifted my foot and took a trembling step into thin air. I cast the speed spell and propelled myself nearly straight down the side of the volcano. Between steps my feet lost traction and for several moments I lifted off the mountain entirely in a stomach-churning free fall. But then my feet found purchase again and I ran on and on, my legs a blur. I plummeted through the clouds, my ears popped, I screamed myself hoarse, and just as suddenly as I'd started, I skidded to a stop, then fell hard on my hands and knees. I rocked back on my heels and turned to look over my shoulder. I dusted off my scuffed hands and righted Iggy's lantern. The ring of clouds had turned black and billowed outward. A glowing orange and black mass skittered down the slopes. Tar was on the move.

My camel had long since run away, but I took a deep breath and cast the speed spell again. I sprinted with everything I had toward Calloon. I had to beat the monster. I had to warn them about Tar.

18

THE ARMOR OF DAMAVASH

I screamed the entire time. My feet flew across the desert, all the way past the camp to the outer walls of Calloon. I skidded to a stop just long enough to catch my breath, and then ran on at my own nonmagical pace out of fear that I'd slam face-first into a wall.

The main square before the palace buzzed with frantic energy. People huddled in little groups and muttered to each other while pointing at the dark smoke that ringed the top of Damavash. Others held their children or their wares and dashed away, their eyes wide with panic.

I dodged them all and burst past the bewildered guards at the main gate of the palace. I pushed between the fronds of two potted palms and stumbled into the middle of Hank and Shaday's wedding ceremony.

I stood at the back of the aisle, panting. The guests sitting closest to me muttered and scooted away. Row by row heads turned until word reached the front where Hank and Shaday stood, a man with a dark mustache and long red and gold robes standing between them. Hank looked so handsome in his formal uniform, with his shiny dark hair combed to the side and his white-gloved hands folded in front of him. Had they said their I do's?

He turned and stared wide-eyed at me. "Imogen."

The hundreds of guests who sat in rows along the aisle grew silent, looking between Hank and me. It was so quiet I could hear the birds chirping in the trees and the gentle trickle of the fountain Hank and Shaday stood before, a canopy covered in blooming white jasmine above them. Fire laced through the fountain—a nod to the combining of their two kingdoms.

"Told ya, pay up." My eyes found Annie standing the hallway off to the side. She held her palm up to Yann and he rolled his eyes and dug around in his tuxedo pocket. Wow. Annie had on lipstick and sequins. In fact, all the bakers stood beside her, other members of the staff watching from the sidelines as well. They all looked fancy and lovely—though Maple blinked at me and Wiley held her shoulders, as if she were about to faint. I gulped. And then it hit me. They thought I was interrupting the wedding to confess my love for Hank. I was going to be the one who spoke now, and did not forever hold my piece.

I spotted Amelia. Her hands balled into fists at her sides, and her mouth hung slack as she stared dumbstruck at me. The gumball-looking device she used to communicate with her team popped out of her ear and rolled across the floor. She didn't even notice.

I held up one hand and shook my head, as my chest heaved and I struggled to catch my breath. I blinked at my fingers—every line and crevice held bits of soot, even the edges of my fingernails. I sniffed and crinkled my nose. What was that smell? Oh, it was me. I still smelled like the clouds of sulfur I'd been in at the top of the volcano.

Hank strode down the aisle toward me, his eyes full of concern. "Imogen, are you all right?"

I shook my head to clear it. "Tar, he's loose." I struggled for breath. "He's coming for the city."

Hank froze and little cries and murmurs rose from the crowd.

"How do you know?" a man cried.

"Get this crazy woman out of here."

In all the hubbub, I somehow found Hank's father's eyes. He stared at me from where he stood in the front row, his eyes hard, and I imagined how Hank must have felt growing up, being looked at that way. Francis hovered nearby in his slim-cut tuxedo.

"I saw him." My chest heaved. Hank closed the gap between us and gripped my arms. "I saw him, slithering down the volcano. He can breathe fire and he's headed for the city."

A wooden chair clunked to the ground as a guest knocked it over in her rush into the palace. Guests stood, their eyes wild, various people shouting conflicting orders to stay put or rush inside for shelter. Hank searched my face and then pulled me against him in a tight hug.

"Thank goodness you're all right," he breathed into the top of my head. "How close were you?" He pulled back and held me at arm's length, looking me over. "Some of your hair has burned off."

My eyes widened. "Oh no." I patted my bun on top of my head and found it crunchy and sharp. "Oh no." I pointed at Hank's white wedding uniform and the Imogen-sized black smudge I'd left down his torso and on both sleeves. "I'm covered in soot." I pressed my hands to my mouth and shook my head. "I've ruined everything."

"Hey." Hank searched my face and used his thumb to

wipe away the tear tracking down my cheek. "No you haven't. You've probably saved more lives than you know."

A deep, vibrating hum rang through the air, then another, then another. Men climbed to the roof and blew in curved ram's horns, sending up the alarm. Half a minute later, more horns answered the call, and then more as word spread across the city. Something in my chest relaxed a little. Maybe there would be time to prepare.

Guests rushed past us. Shaday, radiant in her red-and-gold wedding finery, joined us with Elke at her side. Her mother, father, and two younger brothers were close behind with a several other tribal leaders and royalty behind them, along with Francis. Guards flanked us on all sides and ushered us into the palace. I looked for Maple and the other bakers, but couldn't spot anyone I recognized. Hopefully they'd already gotten inside, and hopefully that afforded us some safety. The guards ushered us past the main hall, which was set with long tables for dinner, where they'd sent all the other guests, and into a smaller room, the royal family's quarters.

Once we were all inside, the guards closed and barred tall wooden doors studded with iron behind us. Shaday and Elke stood together, while the Fire queen Ranita grasped her husband's arm. Hank still held my hand, but I pulled away, since this was still his wedding day after all. He let out a quiet sigh when I took my hand back.

Hank's father strode up to our group with his broad chest puffed out and his shoulders squared. "What is the meaning of all this?" He found me as he looked around the circle and his thick silver brows lowered. "Well, if it isn't the swallow who ruined the Summer Solstice. Come to ruin the wedding now?"

I slid to Hank's side, putting him between us. My heart raced in my chest.

Hank swallowed. "Imogen saved us at the Summer Solstice."

Shaday nodded. "We would have been poisoned."

The king's cold blue eyes never strayed from me. "She certainly likes to make a spectacle of herself."

My stomach turned with nerves. "I had to warn everyone." I swallowed, and found my anger. I *had* saved them. Just because my hair was singed and I smelled of farts didn't mean I deserved to be treated with contempt. "Sorry I didn't have time to freshen up."

Hank kept his expression carefully neutral, but his nostrils flared and his lips twitched, just a hint, toward a smile.

Shaday swept forward, her veils floating around her. She took her father's hands in her own. She stood nearly as tall as him and looked into his dark eyes. "Father, we have to save the city. We cannot just hide in here."

"I'm waiting for word on where the worm is." The Fire King looked left and right, panic lacing his aged features.

She shook her head. "There is no time to wait, if what Imogen says is true." She glanced my way. "And I believe that it is. We need to start up evacuations, using all the airships we can find, and set up shelters in the basements around the city for those who cannot quickly leave. We should form systems at the fountains and pools to source water for putting out fires."

The king nodded. "Those are good ideas." He motioned to one of his councilors and conveyed a few orders to execute Shaday's plans.

"For once, I agree with your daughter."

We all turned, Shaday and her family, Hank and his, to

find Ario Tuk lounging sideways in an expensive-looking winged back chair. I was surprised it hadn't collapsed under his considerable muscled weight.

He kicked his feet. "Not about the evacuations and blah blah blah. About not hiding. This monster must be met head-on." He examined his nails. "If only there were someone brave enough to challenge it to combat." He looked up, revealing the cut on his cheek, and his dark eyes flashed.

One of Shaday's brothers growled, while the other rolled his eyes.

Iggy piped up from the lantern. "Please tell me he's volunteering." He cackled. "I'd like him cooked well-done, please."

Shaday looked bored. "What are you getting at, Ario?"

He pushed himself out of the chair and stomped up to the princess. He stood towering over her, despite her height, and glared down at her. "What I'm getting at is that you need me."

One of Shaday's brothers scoffed.

Ario's lip curled. "Don't talk to your savior that way."

Elke pinched the bridge of her nose.

"Could he be more dramatic?" Iggy moaned.

Ario gripped his white tuxedo shirt in both hands and ripped it apart. Black buttons flew in all directions.

Iggy burst into hysterics. "Oh my goddess, he *can* get more dramatic."

I stifled a chuckle, but the room sobered up as we viewed what lay underneath his shirt. Instead of the thick pelt of chest hair I'd expected him to reveal—well, more like on top of it—black polished leather armor gleamed on his chest. Thick scales, like plates, covered it, just like the monster's skin. I marveled at it. It looked heavy and massive, anyone smaller than Ario would probably have just collapsed under the weight of it.

Queen Ranita gasped. "Damavash's armor."

"Thief!" One of Shaday's younger brothers, in his early twenties, jabbed a finger at Ario. "You stole the armor from the museum!" He rounded on his father. "Have him arrested."

Ario glared with his small dark eyes. "Stole it?" He barked out a humorless laugh. "How could I have? I'm not a shifter and everyone knows a lion took it."

Shaday put a hand on her fuming brother's arm.

Ario lifted his chiseled chin. "It was the decree of the gods that I should have it, just as they gave it to Damavash originally. I am the new hero who shall deliver you all from the wrath of Tar."

Shaday folded her arms.

Ario smirked. "For a price."

"There it is," Elke grumbled.

"What's the import of this armor?" Hank's mother asked no one in particular. She clung to her husband's side.

Queen Ranita answered, her expression solemn. "It allows the wearer an unlimited resistance to huge amounts of fire and heat without being hurt or burned. Or so the legend goes. It's been on display in the museum for ages, no one's tested it."

Ario smirked. "You won't shake my confidence." Several of his men, nearly as beefy as himself, closed rank around Ario, glaring at us all.

Hank's father narrowed his cold blue eyes. They stood out against his tanned skin and silver, close-cropped beard. "And what price are you asking?"

Ario puffed up his broad chest and glared at all the assembled royalty. "I was chosen to receive the armor, just like Damavash, and when I drive the monster back, I should be made king of the Fire Kingdom, just like Damavash."

Shaday's brother lunged forward as if to strike Ario, but Shaday and her other brother held his arms and kept him back. The king's face clouded. He exchanged a grim look with his wife, Queen Ranita.

Francis drifted forward, the toes of his shiny black oxfords dangling a couple of inches above the tiled floor. He cocked his head and looked at Ario with his jet-black eyes. "I could simply take the armor from him." He flashed his fangs.

Ario paled somewhat but jutted his chin out. "If he tries, you'll have a tribal war on your hands."

Shaday gripped her father's shoulder as he slumped under the weight of all the stress.

A knock came at the massive, bolted doors and the guards ushered in a messenger who panted, red-faced and out of breath.

"What news?" Shaday rushed to him.

"The fire snake—" The servant huffed and wiped his forehead. "He's nearly at the wall to the city and coming fast."

"You saw him?" Shaday asked.

The servant dipped his head. "Yes, Princess. He is orange and black with fire and char, screaming flames and tearing up the hard-packed earth with his sharp claws."

Shaday paled and the room grew quiet. She thanked the servant and he bowed before exiting. Her father, King Benam, turned to Ario. "I—I will not bargain with you when it is our kingdom and our people's lives that lie in the balance." He nodded. "I accept your offer. You, or whoever, drives the fire monster back, shall become ruler of the kingdom, and my wife and I will step down from the throne." He patted his wife's hand.

Ario beamed.

Hank's father, King Roch, stepped forward. "The Water Kingdom bears witness to this contract." He stared at the Fire King. "If Ario defeats the snake and becomes ruler, our contract is void and the wedding is off. I won't have my son marrying a commoner."

I let out a breath I hadn't known I was holding. So Hank and Shaday *hadn't* said their vows. They weren't married, yet.

The fire king's throat bobbed, but he nodded his agreement. "Come then, Ario, to the wall. There's no time to waste."

19

THE BATTLE

Within minutes we arrived at the wall to the city. Hank had begged me to stay behind, safe, but I wouldn't have it. I'd been right next to the monster on top of the volcano, though he didn't know that yet. I'd be all right behind the walls of the city. Besides, I didn't want to leave his side.

We stood three stories up on the sand-colored brick walls that surrounded the city. Hank and I linked arms, while Iggy hung in the lantern on my other side. A breeze whipped through the tendrils of my hair that had fallen loose of the bun. All of the royalty and their guards stood in a line beside us, watching as Ario Tuk strode forward from the wall to meet the fire snake.

Though the entrance to the city had once held an iron portcullis, it hadn't been necessary in decades and had fallen into disrepair. Ario was all that stood between the monster and entrance to the city. I glanced behind me.

Down below, people flooded the streets of Calloon. Most followed the shouted orders of the royal guards, who ushered them to the airship landing to be evacuated. Others moved to underground shelters. I sighed. Part of me wished Maple was here with me, selfishly, but another part of me felt grateful that she was in the palace, safe, or being led out of the city. She and my other friends would be all right. I turned back to face the desert, Damavash Volcano in the distance. A plume of dust and black smoke billowed up from where the clawed reptilian monster tore across the sand toward us.

"It's fast," I muttered.

"You were faster." Hank squeezed my arm. "What were you doing out at the camp, though?"

My stomach twisted. He assumed I'd been out where we'd had the feast and spotted the monster from there, not that I was up on the top of the volcano with the man who'd set the monster on the city in the first place.

"Never mind." Hank gave me a tight-lipped smile. "We'll talk later." He looked toward the desert. "When this is all over."

I gulped. If we survived it. But Ario had the magical armor and Damavash had used it in the legends to defeat Tar. Surely Ario would do the same... right?

My breath caught as the monster came clearly into view. It scrambled forward, moving in a strange flopping, dragging, slithering motion. Dust and smoke followed it. Down below, Ario threw his head back and bellowed, thumping his chest with the spear he held in his hand.

"Do we really have to watch this?" Iggy grumbled from the lantern in my hand.

The fire monster answered with a scream that sent chills up my spine. The creature roared like a jet engine, the sound morphing into a guttural noise as though it were about to vomit. I pressed a hand to my stomach.

"Actually, this might be worth watching." Iggy shifted

forward to peer out his lantern. "Go, lizard, go! Bite his head!"

I shot him a look.

Beside Hank, Elke and Shaday conferred, their heads close together. I noticed that they'd made a quick detour in the palace before we left and I spotted one of Elke's patented fire resistant gloves poking out of the bag she wore slung across her chest. So, we had a plan B, apparently.

I squeezed Hank's arm tighter as the monster scrabbled up to Ario. It closed in on him and Ario stepped forward in slow, stomping steps. Hank pressed a fist to his mouth and I held my breath as the two collided. Both figures disappeared from view in the clouds of sand and black smoke that rose around them. Screams from the monster and bellows from Ario rose up. At least he was still alive. Cheers rose up from all around us and I looked about. All along the wall, citizens stood cheering for their hero, and people had even pushed past the guards and stood outside the walls to get a better look. My stomach twisted. They should be evacuating or hiding. Then again, I was right here with them.

"Ar-i-o! Ar-i-o!" people cheered, pumping their fists in the air.

"These people should be getting to safety," Shaday grumbled to Hank.

He nodded his agreement. But apparently the spectacle of the epic battle was too alluring to pass up. Half the city seemed to be watching with us.

And then the dust settled somewhat and revealed a frightening scene. Ario lay supine in the dust, shielding his face with his thick forearms. The monster stood nearly atop him. Its black-plated tail thrashed and it screamed a torrent of fire square at Ario's chest, over and over again. The armor did its job, as Ario appeared unhurt, but the cheering crowd gradually quieted. Why wasn't he getting back up and fighting? The monster kept him pinned down with the constant stream of fire, and then snapped at him with its massive, pointed jaws.

I gasped as Ario fended it off with his spear. The monster hissed, thrashed its tail once more, then turned away from Ario and faced the city.

"Get up," Hank muttered under his breath. "Get up."

But Ario just lay there. He tried to roll right, but couldn't get over. Then he tried left. I pressed a hand to my mouth. "He's stuck. The armor's too heavy, he's like a turtle on its back."

A wheezing noise came from the lantern and I lifted it to find Iggy laughing so hard, barely any noise came out. I dropped him back down to hang at my hip and huffed. I turned to Hank. "What do we do now?"

The citizens of Calloon who'd poured from the city to watch now tripped over themselves and each other to get back inside the city walls. Those next to us on the wall cried out in panic. The monster ignored Ario's shouts of challenge, issued while still lying flat on his back, and tore toward the city. Shaday dug around in Elke's bag and yanked the net-like gloves over her hands and arms.

"Shaday, what are you doing?" Hank's shoulders hiked with stress.

Her nostrils flared. "I'm defending my city."

"We're helping," I piped up from Hank's side.

She nodded. "Fine. Get these other people out of here and to safety."

"What about you?" I asked.

Elke shoved on some fire-resistant gloves and grabbed a shimmering, silky veil from the bag, then handed another one to Shaday. "We're going to give my inventions the ultimate test." She grinned and Shaday gave her a hurried peck on the cheek as they suited up.

Shaday's mother rushed up and grabbed her arm. "What are you doing? Now's no time for dance—we have an airship ready, we're leaving now."

Shaday embraced her mother, then pulled back. "No, Mama. I'm defending my city."

"Why?" She gasped, looking her and Elke over like they were insane. "You'll be killed."

Shaday lifted her beautiful chin. "I'm stronger than you know." She grabbed Elke's hand and pulled her to the nearest stairway, the royal guards helping to create a path for the two down through the shuffling crowds that were rushing to escape.

"Shaday!" her mother screamed at her back.

Hank and I exchanged looks. His blue eyes blazed.

"We can help them." I gulped. "As swallows, we can create bubbles of safety. I don't know for how long or if they'll stand up to the monster's fire blasts, but we can try."

Hank gazed about at the churning mass of people swarming in panic around and below us. "Help the people, or Shaday and Elke?"

I shook my head. "I don't think we're strong enough to protect all of Calloon. But if we protect Shaday and Elke, they might be able to drive it back and save everyone." The wall shuddered and I screamed and fell against Hank. He stumbled back but caught me and kept us upright.

"The monster's through!" a man screamed.

"Son." Hank's father rushed up, his mother and the rest of Hank's brothers and their wives standing behind him, surrounded by tens of guards. Francis hovered beside him. "Come. Our airship is ready for takeoff. We're leaving."

Hank's blue eyes widened. "We can't just leave the Fire Kingdom to deal with this alone."

The king's eyes narrowed. "She's not your wife. And she'll likely not even be a princess when this is all over—*if* she even survives. You owe her nothing."

My jaw dropped. How could he be so cold and calculating?

Hank lifted his chin. "She's not my wife, but she is my friend. And regardless, these are people in need. There's not enough airships for everyone. And what about the hospitals? I'm not leaving them."

Hank's mother sobbed but his father sneered, his eyes full of contempt. "Do as you will."

He spun and the whole family swept away, none of his brothers even bothering to say goodbye. His mother called out and waved and sobbed, but all of her noise and words didn't amount to much. None of them stayed behind to help, except for Francis. But Hank's father turned, glared at our vampire friend, and jerked his head. Francis's face darkened, and I froze. I'd never found him frightening before that moment.

"I have to obey. Good luck." Francis turned and followed behind Hank's family.

Hank blinked and looked away, his eyes glassy. His throat bobbed.

I threw my arms around him. "You're a brave, good man. You deserve a better family."

He hugged me back and kissed the top of my head. "I love you." He jerked and jumped back.

"What?"

"The lantern was getting a bit hot against my backside."

I grimaced. "Sorry. Kinda forgot I was still holding Iggy."

My flame sighed. "Story of my life. And not a side of Hank I'd like to see again, thank you."

I grinned. "Aw, but it's one of his best."

Hank blushed.

"Giant fire monster destroying the city," Iggy reminded us.

I jumped. "Right."

Hank grabbed my hand and we rushed down the stairs, the going painfully slow as we crowded in behind sobbing, screaming, panicked citizens. Finally we reached ground level and found it even worse down below. The monster had breached the wall, but not very far. Buildings all around us burned, and the alarm horns blew from all over the city rooftops. I lurched as someone ran hard into me and didn't even stop.

"Ow."

Hank hugged me close to him, then dragged me to the side as the monster's tail swiped by. We barely dodged it as it screamed, black smoke billowing from the length of its body. Hank pulled me down a side street and a few citizens scrambled past us. I coughed, nearly choking on the sulfurous fumes. Shaday and Elke came into view at the end of the narrow street. They whirled their magical veils in front of them, deflecting a blast of fire, and staggered backward under the force and out of sight. I pressed a hand to my mouth in awe and fear for them. Next came the lizard. Its head came into view between the buildings, its pointed mouth opened wide and spewing fire indiscriminately. Windows shattered and the businesses at the end of the street caught fire. It slithered and wriggled deeper into the city, its blackened body sliding past us. It had to be thirty feet long. Hank and I nodded at each other and then dashed to our right, heading to the next street over in hopes of catching up with Shaday and Elke to help however we could. We rounded the corner of the next street over and sprinted down it, past crates and barrels.

Shaday and Elke came into view, working furiously to drive the monster back. It shot a stream of fire out its mouth and Shaday spun her veil, deflecting it. Then she raised an arm and pulled water from a nearby steaming barrel. The water floated midair in a clear, shifting glob before she hurled it into the monster's red-orange eyes. It hissed and screamed and scrambled back. *Nice one!* We'd nearly reached them when a stream of fire caught Elke unprepared and knocked her to the ground. Her blonde waves splayed all around her head and her fire-resistant veil flew out of her hands.

"Elke!" Shaday whirled around.

The creature took a gasping breath and just as it let loose a deluge of fire, Shaday jumped in front of Elke and held her veil up as a shield. Only instead of knocking the fire aside, the veil took a direct and sustained hit. As Hank and I ran on, our feet scuffing along the dusty mud bricks of the road, the veil smoked and caught fire. I shot my palms out, felt for the energy of the fire monster and pulled from it. But just as I felt full of energy and ready to send magic to Shaday's veil to strengthen it, it disintegrated to ash. I cried out as the fire stream burned directly against Shaday's outstretched palms. She screamed and writhed. With a grunt, I sent a magic bubble out to protect her, imagining the one I'd created atop the volcano. Magic shimmered around her, visible only because the flames the monster spat curved around it, keeping Shaday and Elke safe inside. Sweat beaded on my forehead as I struggled to keep the bubble strong, and then Hank joined me and funneled magic to it, lightening my load.

Shaday collapsed beside Elke and held her wrists against her chest. Her face contorted in pain, and even through the curtain of flames that poured around the bubble of protection, I could see the tears trickling from her eyes. But then Elke stirred, shook her head, and propped up on her elbow. She looked around with wild eyes, taking in everything, and gingerly held Shaday's burned hands in her own.

"She's healing her," Hank ground out, a vein popping out in his neck as he concentrated his magic. "She'll be okay. We have to keep this up as long as we can."

I gritted my teeth and nodded.

"Come on, Imogen." Iggy's lantern swung from one hand. "You can do this!"

Elke scrambled to her feet and helped Shaday up by tugging under her arms. We all skittered backward as Tar charged. His tail swung left and right, knocking holes in buildings and toppling vendors' carts. He screamed and I winced, not sure I'd ever be able to hear again. Though long-term hearing loss was the least of my problems. Elke and Shaday used the multiplier spell to create doppel-gangers of themselves. Their little army twirled and dove and confused the monster, so that he fired at their mirages.

All five Shadays called back over their shoulders. "We need to put out his fire." She spun at the last moment and rolled to the side of a fiery blast. Tar roared like a jet engine.

"We need water." Hank's face had turned beet red from the heat and the effort. He gritted his teeth.

"The fountain!" Elke and her doubles took a flying leap. She landed and rolled to the side of one of Tar's swiping claws. "In the main square."

Working together, Hank funneled magic into the protective bubble while I shifted my effort to fueling Elke and

Shaday so they could continue to use the multiplier spell. We moved backward, luring Tar after us. As we neared the main square, screams and shouts came from more and more citizens. Apparently, lots of people had gathered here and now they scattered as the monster broke free of the streets. His claws punctured the mud-bricked ground and the citizens of Calloon scattered in all directions.

"It's the princess," a woman behind me shouted. I edged backward, sweat pouring from my brow. I blinked to clear my vision. The sun had begun to set and the orange glow of the late afternoon bouncing off the buildings only added to feeling that the entire city was burning.

Shaday took a heaving breath. "Citizens! Come together." She and her doubles twirled right. The monster obliterated one of her illusions with his flames. "Douse it with water!" She screamed to be heard over the monster's cries.

A woman on the edge of my vision lifted her arms and hurled an undulating glob of liquid forward. But instead of hitting the monster, it hit Shaday. She jerked, but then grinned. She gleamed with oil. I gasped—it was the protective oil she'd described the women using for their fire dances. The woman had helped her. Another woman and another stepped forward and threw more of the oil on Elke and Shaday from a distance. Little by little, more help arrived, and soon it seemed as though water and oil flew from all sides of the square.

The monster jerked and writhed as steam rose up from its body. It turned blacker and blacker as the glowing orange cracks between its charred scales shrunk.

My chest heaved with exhaustion. I glanced at Hank. "It's working."

He panted and flashed a quick grin. Then we both turned back and concentrated on protecting Shaday and

Elke. I pulled my magical energy from the monster itself, hoping to weaken him by doing so. It took nearly half an hour of combined, concentrated effort, but bit by bit the monster shrunk down and cooled until he shriveled to only the size of a large iguana. He still snapped his jaws and swung his tail, but his blasts of fire diminished to the point that Elke rushed forward, threw her surviving veil over him, and smothered his fire.

Shaday marched forward. She held her arms out to a royal guard who stood nearby, and he tossed her his spear. She caught it but winced and dropped it. It clanked to the ground. Her hands must've been burned pretty badly when she shielded Elke from that blast. Instead she held her hands out, ready to cast a spell and destroy the creature.

But just before she did, someone cried out. "Ssstop."

I whirled to see Sam running across the square from the palace, with Maple, Wiley, and the other bakers on his heels. My chest heaved as I swayed on my feet. My friends were okay.

Shaday hesitated.

"It'sss not hisss fault." Sam ran closer, his arms swinging loosely at his sides. "He'sss jussst a creature. Ssssomeone ssset him on the cccity, but he wasss being usssed. Don't kill him." Sam blinked his big blue eyes.

Shaday's brows drew together.

A man nearby scoffed. "He's killed and wreaked havoc on the city. Kill it, before it rises up and destroys all of us."

Shouts of agreement rose up from the crowd that slowly moved in around us. Faces appeared in windows around the square and people wandered out of their hiding places. Shaday licked her lips and glanced around. A nasty pink burn streaked across her cheek and she seemed unable to open one eye.

My mouth dropped. "Shaday, you need medical attention."

Elke threw an arm around the princess as she debated.

Sam clasped his hands together. "Pleassse."

Shaday panted and her shoulders slumped. She dropped her arms to her sides. "Contain it. Douse it with more water to bring it even smaller. We'll sort out what to do with it later."

"Thhhank you," Sam gasped.

Huh. Go Sam, standing up for what he believed in. But having just battled the creature, to be honest, I wasn't feeling as charitable as Shaday toward it.

Murmurs sounded from the crowd. Shaday staggered and Elke steadied her. "Just because we don't understand something doesn't mean we should destroy it. What Sam said is true. The monster was just a tool—we must seek justice with whoever wielded him on us." Her head rolled to her chest and Elke cried out as Shaday collapsed. Guards and citizens rushed forward to catch her. A small crowd rushed her across the square to the palace infirmary.

20

A NEW KIND OF KING

One of the Fire King's councilors raised his arms and again called for quiet. No one paid him any attention. The main hall of the riad churned with activity, packed to the brim with visiting royalty in town for the wedding, rulers of the other Fire Kingdom tribes, and regular citizens of Calloon. The tables and chairs for the wedding reception had been cleared out or stacked against the walls. The rest of the city packed into the main square, waiting to hear what came of this emergency meeting.

It had only been an hour since we'd stood just outside the palace and battled a giant fire monster. My stomach twisted when I thought of Shaday. She, her mother, and Elke still weren't back from the infirmary, and we'd heard nothing. I clasped my hands tightly in my lap and hoped Shaday would be all right. I'd seen a glimpse of her hands and forearms. The skin had stretched tight and pink and gnarled over her charred fingers—burned when she'd shielded Elke from that direct blast of fire that would surely have killed her.

Hank sat beside me in his own chair, both of us too exhausted to stand, with Iggy in a lantern at my feet. Hank slid his warm hand around mine and gave my fingers a squeeze. His mother, father, and eldest brother, Michael, and his wife milled about on the raised platform where we sat at one end of the main hall. They spoke with Shaday's father and brothers and a variety of councilors and heads of tribes. Francis hovered nearby.

I leaned forward. "We're out of our league," I muttered to Iggy as I glanced around at all the glittering jewels and crowned heads around us.

Iggy scoffed. "Speak for yourself."

Maple and the rest of the bakers, along with Rhonda, stood toward the back of the room. I'd only gotten VIP stage seating because of my connection to Hank... and also possibly because I'd helped defeat the monster.

Again, one of the councilors looked out over the tightly-packed crowd of bodies and called for order, shouting to be heard over the deafening cacophony of voices. He turned and gave an annoyed shake of his head. Amelia strode forward and motioned to a nearby guard, who handed her the curved ram's horn at his belt. I recognized it as one of the ones used to call out the alarm from the rooftops. Hank and I exchanged wide-eyed glances and then pulled our hands apart to plug our ears. Amelia put the horn to her lips and blew. The deep, reverberating sound vibrated in my chest and shocked the crowd. They jumped and put their hands over their ears, turning wide-eyed toward Amelia and the rest of us behind her. Amelia dropped the horn to her side and huffed.

"The meeting will now begin. We require your full attention and"—she raised a finger—"your silence until it is your turn to speak."

Voices immediately called out a variety of questions.

"We want answers!"

"My house burned, who will pay for it?"

"Is the monster going to return?"

Amelia opened her eyes wide in warning and brought the horn back to her lips. The crowd quieted. She sniffed and hugged the horn to her. "I'm going to hold on to this." She swept an arm out. "King Benam, the floor is yours." Amelia stepped back as Shaday's father stepped forward, his back to Hank and me, and faced his people.

"I know you have many questions and I shall strive to answer them as best I can." His shoulders slumped.

"Was it Tar?" a woman in the crowd shouted.

The king bowed his head and then answered. "I do not know. The creature certainly resembled the way Tar is described in the legends."

"Is he still a danger?" a man called up from the back.

The king squared his shoulders. The flickering light of wall torches glinted off his gold robes. "No. Thanks to the brave actions of many of our soldiers and citizens, as well as to our guests Prince Harry of the Water Kingdom and his friend, Imogen Banks." He swept an arm toward us and my cheeks burned hot as hundreds of eyes gazed at me and Hank. "But most of my gratitude goes to my daughter, Shaday, and her friend Elke, who so bravely fought the creature back." The king's voice broke at the end and murmurs ran through the crowd.

"Where is she?"

Her father shook his head. "Shaday is being treated for burns and we are awaiting word of her condition."

Cries and concerned voices clamored together and Hank and I exchanged worried glances. At that moment, the big iron-studded wood doors at the back of the hall opened, letting in a waft of cool night breeze scented with orange blossoms. The king stiffened, and people jostled and shoved and cried out at the back of the hall. I leaned forward and squinted. What was happening? The crowd gradually parted to form an aisle down the center of the long room. They bowed and curtsied deeply as Shaday strode past, supported at each arm by her mother and Elke.

I sucked in a breath and lurched out of my seat, Hank right beside me. I smiled as tears filled my eyes. She was all right—all right enough to walk, even. White bandages wrapped her hands and arms to her elbows and her normally golden skin looked green, but she was alive. As Shaday approached, all the others on the stage beside me, including her father, dropped into bows. I folded at the waist as well, certain that my legs would buckle if I attempted a curtsy.

We rose and Shaday's father reached a hand down and gently helped his daughter up the few steps to the raised platform, where he embraced her. The crowd erupted into applause, clapping and whooping and whistling.

After embracing her brothers and waving at the crowd, Shaday turned to us. "I'm so glad you two are all right." Though black bags hung under her eyes, she grinned. "We did it."

I reached out to squeeze her hand but froze when I remembered the bandages. I gulped. "Your hands, are they...?"

Shaday pressed her lips together. "They're painful, but the healers say I should regain full use of them. Eventually."

My stomach sunk.

Elke shook her head, her golden waves bouncing over her shoulders. How did her hair look so good after the day we'd had? "I told her she needs to stop minimizing her injuries. Her hands are burned, and badly. It will take many treatments over many months, years maybe, to heal them. And even then they will be scarred." She shook her head sadly.

Shaday nudged her shoulder against Elke's. "Yes, they'll be scarred, but nothing some new tattoos won't cover up." She lifted her chin and stood tall.

I shook my head. "Shaday, I have to tell you, I am in awe."

"That makes two of us." Hank pressed his lips together. "If there's anything I can do to help—perhaps send you our kingdom's best healers to see if they have any complementary treatment ideas? And we will definitely send aid to help you rebuild Calloon."

Shaday bowed her head. "I appreciate it, thank you. As for the city, the hospital survived, thank the flames, and the first phase of recovery has already begun. We've organized more treatment centers around the city, and have recruited volunteers to deal with the fires." She blew out a breath. "Also, the head curator from the Royal Artifacts Museum is apparently a huge Legend of Damavash fan and has promised to look through all of his materials to discover the spell from the story that might seal the monster in the volcano for good." She lifted a shoulder. "In any case, the monster will be contained."

I frowned. "As in, you've arranged this in the last hour from your hospital bed?"

Elke rolled her eyes. "She's so stubborn. Her mother and I both urged her to rest, but she doesn't listen."

Shaday's eyes flicked to the ceiling and back down. "Since when did you and my mother gang up against me?" She looked at Hank. "We'll talk soon and settle everything."

Queen Ranita swept up to us in her flowing gown. "Shaday, the people need to hear from you. And your father has some words to say. Come."

Shaday followed and nodded to Elke to join her. Elke paled, but squared her shoulders and they both turned around to face the impatient, murmuring crowd.

Shaday's father raised his arms. "I would like to officially honor my daughter, Shaday, and her friend Elke Beckham for the bravery and skill they showed in successfully defending our city from the hideous monster that attacked us." The crowd broke into applause and I clapped enthusiastically along with them. Hank joined in, and Iggy whistled from the lantern.

A scowling man shoved his way forward. "How'd she know how to do that?" He shouted his question at Shaday's father.

Her mother lifted a dark brow and muttered, "That is something I would like to know as well."

Shaday gulped.

The man narrowed his eyes. "Have you been training your females in combat?" He sneered. "It is not their place."

Some cheers and some boos rang out from the crowd. I bristled and clenched my hands into fists. "She saved us all, how can he say that?"

Hank set his jaw and shook his head. "I don't know."

Shaday lifted her chin. "Elke here, daughter of the late Bernhardt Beckham, has been my tutor in their unique method of hand-to-hand combat. But combined with my dance training, we have created our own style of fighting." The crowd muttered, surprised. "And Elke's inventions, gloves and veils made from new type of fabric she has created, were instrumental in our ability to fight off the creature." She narrowed her eyes and her lip curled as she looked down on the angry man. "But if you'd have preferred us to stay in the sewing room and let the monster eat your children and burn you alive, then my apologies for acting out of place."

That got some laughs, but the man growled and was joined by angry shouts from other male voices.

"All these years?" Shaday's mother muttered.

The princess turned to her, her face sober. "Mama. This is me. I know you've always wanted an elegant, quiet girl, and I've tried to be that." She shook her head, her eyes welling with tears. "But this is who I've always been. I think deep down you know that."

The queen's chin quivered, and her eyes grew glassy, but she kept her lips pressed firmly together and said nothing.

As the crowd grew more raucous, Elke stomped her heeled foot and planted her hands on her curvy hips. "This your princess. She risked exposing the secret of her combat training, risked more than that, her very life, to save you, her people and her city. Her hands are forever scarred from this! She literally beat back a fire monster for you!" The crowd listened, wide-eyed. "What more could you ask for in a warrior and a ruler?" She spun to Shaday's father. "She has earned the right to the crown."

Gasps sounded among the crowd and Queen Ranita's mouth hung open. But Shaday's father stepped forward and embraced his daughter.

"The king, under witness, promised the crown to whoever defeated the fire monster!" Elke shouted to be heard over the jumbled shouts and cheers and boos from the crowd. She threw her arm toward Shaday. "Even if she weren't the eldest, she has earned the right to rule today with her heroics!"

Though deep voices of disagreement and discontent threaded through the crowd, the majority of the people erupted into applause. I smiled, surprised and pleased that her people would accept Shaday as their queen—most of them, at least. Hank and I grinned at each other. The applause bounced off the marble-tiled floors and walls and grew deafening as Shaday dipped her chin and her father lifted the gold-pointed crown from his head and set it upon Shaday's dark one. The red center ruby glinted in the fire-light from the torches, and appeared to burn. Apt for the princess who'd destroyed a monster made of fire.

She lifted her face and the applause grew louder, though I hadn't thought it possible. Her father embraced her again, and when Shaday turned to face her mother, the queen burst into tears and threw her arms around her daughter. Shaday awkwardly wrapped her bandaged arms around her mother's back and tears flowed from my eyes.

As the crowd quieted and Shaday gazed lovingly at Elke, who'd stood up for her and now stood beside her, the big wooden doors at the back of the hall opened again, shoving the people who stood near them to the side. Ario Tuk strode in and I gritted my teeth.

"He has some nerve," Hank ground out.

Even from a distance, I could make out the sneer on Ario's face. "If you think I or any of my people will bow to *her*," he bellowed, "you're delusional! You have just lost the following of the tribes." Tens of burly men surrounded him and shouted their agreement.

21

A PROPOSAL

As Queen Ranita stepped forward, her skirts swirled around her ankles. She edged between Shaday and Ario and his men who shouted protests. "You'd *better* learn to bow. She's your queen now!"

Shaday murmured, "Thanks, Mama." She spoke loud enough for her voice to carry across the long hall. "I don't blame you for refusing to bow. The armor you so dubiously obtained might cause you to tip forward and fall flat again." She lifted her bandaged arms in the air. "Imagine if someone willing to fight had had the benefit of fireproof magic."

Laughter and cheers boomed through the hall, but Ario and his supporters shoved their way forward, knocking people to the ground. Royal soldiers clamored forward to meet the men, but Shaday stayed them with a shake of her head. They paused, tensed and waiting for orders around the perimeter of the huge room.

Ario sneered. "Very noble of you, to mock a man who met a monster head-on and was injured in the effort." His dark eyes glinted.

Elke narrowed her eyes and watched him closely, her head tilted to one side.

Hank stepped forward. "You haven't a scratch on you. And once you were helped back up to your feet again, then what? You could have joined us in the fight. You gave up because you lost your chance to look like a hero." He looked out at the crowd. "Fire Kingdom, you have a choice—you can have a woman who risked everything to save you, or a man who walked away from the fight because of a bruised ego."

The crowd cheered again, and Ario and his supporters grumbled and glared, but shuffled closer together, outnumbered.

"We will follow her." I searched the crowd until I spotted the speaker, Lilya, the servant I'd followed to the underground meeting. She raised her fist in the air, her half-moon tattoo visible on her wrist. "It's about time women had some rights around here." A huge group around her threw their arms in the air and shouted their support. More and more people joined them until the hall rung with cheers, and Ario and his men had nothing to do but scowl and slink back toward the entrance to the hall.

Elke muttered to the councilor nearest her. "Bar the doors. Make sure Ario doesn't leave just yet."

Hank's father surveyed the cheering crowd with his cold, calculating eyes and spoke loudly in his deep, commanding voice. "The Water Kingdom also acknowledges Shaday as queen." He bowed to her and Shaday tilted her head in acknowledgment. I wasn't a fan of King Roch in general, but still, a vote of support. He slid past Hank and stood beside the new queen. "Of course, it has been a difficult day and you will need time for recovery. But today was supposed to be a celebration of marriage, and I hope that we can speak soon to discuss new wedding plans."

My stomach turned. I'd nearly forgotten. In all the relief of surviving the monster attack, I'd forgotten that I shouldn't be completely relieved yet—a huge weight still hung over me.

"There it is."

I frowned and crouched down beside Iggy. "What was that?"

He rolled his eyes. "I'm sure our king is pleased as punch that his least favorite son, who I'm sure he was just marrying off to Shaday to get better camel trade deals with the Fire Kingdom, or something minor, is now going to be married not to a princess who will never rule, but the *actual* queen. Of course he wants to get them married as soon as possible."

My stomach turned. "You're right."

I stood and Hank frowned at me. "Are you okay? You look like you're going to be sick."

I felt like it, too.

Shaday glanced back at me over her shoulder, her eyes twinkling, and winked. My brows shot up. What was she up to? She turned to Hank's father. "You know, I say, why wait?"

King Roch beamed and Hank's shoulders stiffened.

Shaday lifted her bandaged arms and the heads of her people turned to her again. "I have one last thing to say. Today was supposed to be my wedding day." She took a deep breath and the hall quieted. "Obviously, that didn't happen."

Laughs twittered among the crowd.

"But I should like, more than anything, to set a new date for my marriage."

Hank's father clapped a hand on his son's shoulder and shook it. "Never thought you'd be sitting on the throne, eh son?" he muttered. "Not a king, but still, prince consort's not bad, especially for you." I stood close enough to hear. "Never thought you'd be much of anything. A day of surprises." Hank recoiled slightly, his shoulders hunched up, and I had to stop myself from reaching forward and taking his hand.

Shaday turned to Elke and her chest heaved as Elke's eyes widened. "Elke Beckham, will you marry me?"

Elke gasped. I gasped. Shaday's mother covered her mouth.

Shaday's eyes welled with tears. "I'd get down on one knee, but I don't think I could get back up."

Elke laughed, then pressed a hand to her mouth and shook her head, tears trickling down her face. "Now?" Her eyes slid to the dumbstruck crowd. "They might not accept this—us—you."

Shaday grinned. "Who cares? We almost died today. Kinda puts things in perspective."

"Is that a yes, then?" Shaday's mother burst out.

Shaday and Elke turned to her, shock all over their faces. Then they both giggled as Elke nodded, "Yes." The two embraced.

I clasped my hands together. "They're so cute."

Shaday's mother embraced her daughter for a long time, and they both wept. It took the crowd a few moments to catch up, but applause slowly spread among the them, quieter and less raucous then before. But as I looked out over their faces, it didn't appear to be from a lack of enthusiasm, so much as from the realization that the Fire Kingdom was about to change in many big and permanent ways, and that they were witnessing that change right in front of them. Their faces were wide-eyed, and many mouths hung open—but openness was a good thing.

Then I noticed someone who was apparently feeling a little less amenable to the situation. A storm was brewing in

Hank's father's head. Hank's mother cringed back, watching her husband with her brows drawn together in concern. He strode up to Shaday and her family, his face dark and his teeth bared.

"You've broken our contract." His nostrils flared. "Harry was to be your husband. Under the stipulations, if one party ends the engagement, the other is entitled to considerable reparations, and believe me I intend to collect and then some. When I get done—"

Hank brushed past him, his blue eyes flashing. He lifted his chin. "I renounce any claims to reparations from Shaday or her family and accept equal part in ending our engagement."

My jaw dropped. Go Hank!

Hank swiveled toward me and his mouth spread into a grin, despite the fact that his father was turning a dark shade of crimson and a twisted vein bulged at his neck. Hank walked up to me and lowered his voice. "Do you still love me?"

I frowned. "Of course I do, but what—"

He grabbed my hand tight in his own and spun around to face his father, mother, and everyone else. "I *also* end the engagement, because I'm in love with Imogen Banks, and have been for some time now. She's the one I want to be with, and the one I hope to someday marry."

Was this happening? Was this really happening? My eyes found Maple in the crowd. Her mouth formed a round O.

I turned back to Hank. "Are you sure about this?" I held a hand to the side of my mouth. "Your dad doesn't seem too pleased."

"He's never pleased with me." Hank frowned. "Or

anything, actually. And yes, I've never been surer about anything in my life."

He took my face in his hands and kissed me. I forgot about everyone on the stage around us and the rest of the hall packed with hundreds of people. They all faded away and there was just Hank and me, cocooned in a bubble of tingly happiness. Warmth spread through me and I melted into him.

"I hadn't realized how much I'd missed this," I murmured, my lips against his cheek.

"I had, every day." Hank kissed me again and I pulled him into me, my arms wrapped around his muscled waist.

"You're choosing a commoner, a swallow."

The venom in the words made me freeze. Slowly, Hank and I pulled apart, though as we turned we kept our arms around each other.

The king's eyes bulged and he'd turned so red he looked purple. His chest heaved.

"That's me," I said in a small voice.

Shaday and her family watched, tense, their eyes darting between the king and Hank and me. Shaday stepped forward, edging between us. She addressed Hank. "As queen, I would like to take a moment to honor the bravery Hank and Imogen showed in coming to our kingdom's aid. I very much look forward to dealing with *you*, Hank, since we've established such a warm friendship, and I am certain that warmth will extend to the relationship between our two kingdoms." She turned to Hank's father. "In fact, I *insist* on Hank being the emissary from the Water Kingdom to our own." She smiled and tried for a light tone. "I shall look forward to working with him, and will work *only* with him."

The king's eyes flashed as he looked from Shaday to Hank. His nostrils flared. "Very well then. I suppose, in the interest of my kingdom, I will appoint Harry to deal with you and your people." He nodded at Shaday, but his hard eyes slid to me and I fought hard not to take a step back... or to run and go hide for forever. Hank squeezed me closer to his side.

So it was official. Hank and I were publicly together, and his father wanted to kill me... or him... or both of us. I smiled gratefully at Shaday and she winked again. Two winks, I felt honored. And thankful that she'd intervened for us. By only agreeing to deal with Hank, she'd basically ensured that Hank's father couldn't literally kill him or banish him and strip him of his powers, as Hank had feared.

I let out a heavy breath and leaned my head against Hank's shoulder. I could do that anytime time I wanted to now. Happy tingles danced through me from my head to my toes.

22

AN ACCUSATION

S houts turned our attention to the far end of the hall, where Ario and his guys pushed against the crowd of people near the door as they attempted to leave. People cried out in protest as he shoved them to the side.

Elke leaned closer to Shaday. "How did he say he got that armor again?"

Shaday smirked. Then she lifted her chin and called out across the long room, "Stay, Ario. I have some questions for you."

Four guards, clad in crimson robes and leather armor and braces, stepped in front of the studded doors, barring Ario's exit.

He spun. "I will not bow to you," he barked.

"We'll see." Shaday held her bandaged arms at her sides. "But first, I want to know. How did you come to wear Damavash's armor? The same armor stolen from the museum last month."

Even all the way across the hall, his face visibly reddened. The faces of the crowd swiveled toward him.

Those nearest us rose on their toes to see over the heads of the crowd.

"I told you." His dark eyes glinted in the torchlight. "The fabled lion brought it to me, the same lion so many witnessed take the armor from the museum. It was decreed by the gods that I should have it, and"—he jabbed a finger at Shaday—"that I should be the rightful king."

"This guy is the worst," I grumbled.

Hank grinned and nodded his agreement.

But something nagged at me, something about the lion bringing him the armor.

The crowd turned to look toward Shaday. She shook her head, slowly. "I don't believe you, Ario. Because a true leader doesn't bargain with lives and use his people's time of need as a path toward personal gain."

Ario grew redder.

"If there are any gods, they wouldn't have given the armor to you."

He'd sat in a chair, in this very hall, and examined his nails as the monster scrambled toward us. He wasn't in the least alarmed, maybe because he was wearing fireproof armor, but it seemed like more than that. It was as if he'd known the monster was going to be unleashed and was prepared to make that ultimatum—his help, for the throne. But how could he have known that? Horace had been the one who—

My stomach twisted.

As Ario stormed toward Shaday and the rest of us on the stage, shouting at her and shaking his fist, memories flashed through my mind, the pieces coming together. I thought of fluttering around Urs Volker's tent as a moth with Horace waiting outside, following Horace to the dive bar with him disguised as an archaeologist, the scrolls in his bag, and again, he had that bag with him up on the volcano. I pictured Horace, his eyes lit up by the orange blaze of the lava, the smirk on his face. He'd wondered aloud if anyone would be as brave as Damavash and step forward to protect the city.

I shot my hand out and gripped Hank's wrist. He turned to me.

"Imogen?" Hank's brow furrowed.

"It was Ario."

"What was?" Iggy asked from his lantern.

"It was Ario and Horace together." My eyes shifted from side to side as I tried to piece it all together.

"Horace?" Hank recoiled and looked around the hall.

I walked forward and stood beside Shaday, with Elke on her other side. The hall churned in turmoil. Guards clamored to get at Ario as he hurled insults at Shaday, but the men from his tribe shoved them back, and skirmishes broke out among irritated, tired people throughout the hall.

I pointed a trembling arm at Ario. "You killed Bernhardt Beckham."

Elke rounded on me, her eyes wide and face pale. "You're sure of this?"

I pressed my lips together and gave her a tight nod. She turned toward Ario, her eyes blazing and teeth bared.

Ario scoffed. "Absurd. How desperate are you that you resort to accusing me of such a thing?"

My nostrils flared. "How'd you get that scratch on your cheek?"

His sneer dropped, and he pressed a finger to his face.

"From Bernhardt's medal? The attacker's blood was found on it. You put him in a choke hold, your faces close together. The medal he wore at his neck scratched you then, didn't it?"

"How do you know zis?" Urs Volker, surrounded by his black-uniformed officers, stepped closer to the stage, his penetrating blue eyes fixed on me. I really hoped I was right. But there was too much evidence, I had to be. I ignored Urs for now. I'd need to think up some way to excuse how I knew what I knew, but that would have to wait.

"Did you send your servant in first? He was cursed, wasn't he, by the protective spells around the tent and became ill? Yes, there was something going around among the staff, but his illness was violent and different from all the others. When he failed, you had to go in and do the job."

Ario's throat bobbed. He scoffed, though his dark eyes shot murder at me. "Who's going to believe this woman's wild imaginings?"

Elke leaned across Shaday. "How do you know this?"

Shaday lifted a brow. "Do you have proof?"

I grimaced.

"We can't arrest him without proof." Shaday's dark eyes searched my face.

I glanced at her burned and bandaged arms. I couldn't let her fight be for nothing; I couldn't let Ario get away with murder. But that meant I had to tell some things that wouldn't be easy to tell—some secrets I'd promised not to reveal. No one but Iggy knew I'd been in contact with Horace, and only Hank and the bakers knew he was my brother, so I needed to proceed carefully.

I took a deep breath and raised my voice. "Ario worked with Horace, leader of the Badlands Army."

Gasps rang out through the hall. Elke's jaw dropped.

"Horace transformed into a lion and stole the armor." Just like him, too—he probably thought it was poetic. I was beginning to pick up on my brother's trickster tendencies, he liked symbolism and mystery.

"Horace is a shifter?" Shaday lifted a dark brow.

Ario laughed without humor. "This woman is a flaming fool. We all know the museum was heavily guarded against all kinds of magic, including shifters."

I glanced back toward Hank where he stood beside Iggy. He'd paled but gave me a nod of encouragement.

I addressed Ario and the anxious crowd. "Horace is a swallow."

Gasps sounded through the crowd.

"A swallow?"

"What is that?"

I lifted my brows in surprise. Apparently, we *were* rare—so much so that many hadn't even heard the term.

"I am a swallow as well." I lifted my chin to project confidence, though my hands trembled. "We draw our power from without, giving us the ability to perform more powerful spells than the average person."

Hank stepped up beside me and took my hand. Energy and love flowed through me, giving me renewed confidence.

His deep voice cut through the murmur of the crowd. "I too am a swallow and can vouch that what she says about Horace is true."

A choked noise made me spin. Hank's father flushed bright red and his steely blue eyes nearly bulged out of his head. Hank's mother petted his arm and whispered in his ear, no doubt trying to calm him. What was he so upset about? Maybe he didn't like Hank revealing that he was a swallow? I hadn't thought it was a secret... though maybe, like Horace, he hadn't wanted it publicized. My heart pounded as I remembered my brother's change of attitude toward me, the anger, as he left me alone on the volcano with a monster. Would I be a target now? I gulped. He was certainly not going to be happy when he heard about what I was going to say next.

"Horace, as a swallow, has the ability to transform into an animal, like a shifter, but the protective spells against shifters wouldn't have affected him."

Hank frowned down at me. "Are you sure, Imogen? I've never transformed myself or heard of anyone besides a shifter doing so."

I nodded.

"She's lying!" Ario spat.

"I'll prove it." I closed my eyes. The room swirled with the energy of the crowd, but I didn't want to pull from any one person by accident and hurt them. So I found their emotions instead—the anxiety, the hurt, the fear—and pulled from that. Maybe it would calm the mood in the room as a bonus side effect. I pictured a tawny lion with a full mane. I suppose I could have pictured a female lion, but the mane seemed more impressive. A whirlwind of energy blew about me, took me up and set me back down, on all four paws.

Screams rang out through the hall and, just because I could, I raised my fanged mouth and let out a deep roar.

I quickly changed back to myself and found the entire hall stunned, Hank included. His mouth hung open. I winked at him and his eyes widened. I felt pretty pleased with myself for stumping him, as he'd been teaching me so much over the last many months.

"How did you learn to do that?" he whispered, in awe. My stomach sank then. I couldn't exactly answer that Horace had taught me, since he hadn't known we'd been in contact. Didn't feel so pleased with myself at *that* moment. I hoped that Horace had been wrong, and that I wouldn't be despised and discriminated against as much as Sam and other shifters were. I gulped as I looked up at Hank's handsome face. I hoped I hadn't made things difficult for Hank either, especially given his father's reaction. Then again, his father seemed likely to have a conniption about everything I had to say or do.

Ario's lip curled. "So what? She can turn into a lion. Maybe this *Horace* can, too." He sniffed. "But I don't know any Horace."

Urs raised his voice so that the whole hall could hear, but addressed me. "Blueprints vere shtolen from Bernhardt's tent. Vhy vould *he* vant them?" He jerked his head towards Ario.

The rolled papers in his bag—Horace had had the blueprints on him when he went through the portal mirror. I took a breath and made sure I had it clear in my head. "He didn't. My guess is that Horace planned to unleash the monster, Tar, on the city and told Ario about his plans."

Ario paled.

"He knew Ario wanted the throne and made him a deal. If Ario brought Horace the blueprints of Carclaustra Prison, Horace would give him the armor of Damavash. Ario used that armor to negotiate for the throne, in exchange for defeating the monster, as he knew he'd be the only one who could." I glanced at Shaday and Elke. "At least, he *thought* he was the only one who could."

Urs turned his hard eyes on Ario. "And I'm sure za leader off oon terrorist organization, zome off whose members are incarcerated een za prison, can sink of many uses for such blueprints."

I thought of Pritney and Nate, who'd both claimed to be very close to Horace. I'd sent them to Carclaustra by foiling their plans.

"Horace is planning something," Hank mused.

I nodded. "Definitely."

Elke frowned. "But why wouldn't Horace have just stolen the blueprints for himself? If he can turn into a lion and steal armor from the museum, why would he need help getting the blueprints?"

I nodded. I'd thought of that myself. But when I'd turned into a moth and spied on Urs, Horace had stayed behind. I narrowed my eyes. As if he *couldn't* enter the tent. And Urs had been in charge of casting the protective spells around Bernhardt's tent as well, meaning he'd probably used the same spells for his tent. "My guess is there was some very specific spell around the tent that prevented him from entering." I shrugged. "Additionally, I think he enjoys sowing chaos. He probably loved creating turmoil within the kingdom over the throne."

Urs gave a grave nod of his head. "I cannot disclose za details, as eet ees a high-level security secret, but zis young voman ees correct. Rest assured, Horace vould haf been avare off certain shpells zat vould haf prevented him entering za tent heemself."

"So he sent this coward, Ario." Elke's eyes shot daggers at him.

I shook my head. "Well, this coward likely sent his servant first, who got ill and failed. So he went himself, and Bernhardt let him in. They probably shared some wine, Bernhardt got drunk, and Ario hoped to sneak out with the blueprints. Only I bet Bernhardt noticed, Ario panicked, and he killed him."

Ario's chest heaved and his small dark eyes darted left and right, like a cornered animal's. "All guesses. There is no evidence!"

Urs Volker shot him a heavy look. "Ve'll see what your servant has to say about zat."

Ario paled, then sneered, then paled again and turned and ran for the doors. People shouted and screamed as he shoved them aside and lumbered toward the exit.

"Stop him!" Shaday commanded.

Her guards blocked the doorway while others, including Urs's security officers, closed in around him. It took three Fire Kingdom guards, but they tackled him to the ground and bound him with magic. It probably wasn't necessary. We'd seen that the armor was too heavy for him to get up, anyway.

Shaday hugged Elke to her and they both turned to me, sad smiles on their faces. Elke shook her head slightly. "Thank you, Imogen, for catching my father's killer. We didn't see eye to eye on much, but he didn't deserve to be murdered."

I nodded, my lips in a tight smile.

Urs Volker turned to Shaday. "Vee haf room for heem een Carclaustra, eef you decide to punish heem een zat vay."

She dipped her chin. "Thank you. I'll keep that in mind."

Urs bowed and then moved toward the exit with his officers to help escort Ario away.

23

BRAVE

The meeting concluded, and Amelia and the councilors worked to usher the gathered crowd out of the hall and either back home, or to the hospital or whatever aid service they might need.

I grabbed Iggy, then turned to Hank and we smiled at each other. Hank took my free hand and we followed Shaday, Elke, and the rest of the royal families out a back exit, through the palace, up some winding tiled stairs, and finally out into the cool night air. The smell of smoke and burned wood hung heavy in the air, and black plumes of smoke darkened the night sky, outlining the path the monster had taken through the city. Hank and I moved, hand in hand, to the edge of the roof and stood with the others in a line to look down on the enormous crowd gathered in the main square.

Despite all the fear and destruction, the city had faced earlier, the people were ready to celebrate their victory over the monster, and their new queen who'd saved them. Shaday lifted her bandaged arms and the crowd of tightly packed bodies below erupted into deafening applause. A huge smile stretched over my face.

"Wow. They love her."

Hank put an arm around me and hugged me close. "She's going to be a good queen."

I nodded and snuggled against him. So much had just changed between us. A future actually seemed possible. Happiness rushed through me.

"I hope it's all right that I made our relationship public?"

I looked up into Hank's pinched eyes. My lips quirked to the side. "I was surprised, and I don't think your dad's too happy about it." I glanced to my left, past Hank's eldest brother and his wife to the king and queen of the Water Kingdom. Hard lines etched the king's tanned face—everything about the man seemed hard. I smiled back at Hank, so honorable and kind. How had he turned out so well? "But I love you, and while I'm sure there will be some new challenges..." I took a deep breath and let it out. "I'm so relieved that it's not a secret anymore. And for the first time in a long time I feel hopeful."

Hank bent his face to mine and kissed me. His large hand cupped my chin and he slid the fingers of his other through my hair. He spoke against my ear. "I can't imagine living without you. I came so close to that today..."

I nuzzled against him. "From the wedding or the us almost not living at all because of the monster part?"

He chuckled and I felt the rumblings of it in his chest against mine. "Both. Imogen, I won't let that happen again."

"Good." I kissed him again, and while our lips were together, everything seemed right in the world.

POP! We jumped apart. *POP!* Fireworks streaked through the sky in gold and red starbursts. An enchanted one exploded, and depicted Shaday fighting off a flaming monster, their images stretched out across the night sky and the stars.

As we watched the show, I glanced up at Hank. The colorful light bounced off his strong jaw, straight large nose, and his lively eyes.

He caught me watching and dipped down to whisper in my ear. "I'm so impressed with you."

POP! The exploding fireworks made it difficult to talk.

"Later, I want to hear all about how you put that together and solved the murder, and how you were able to warn us. You were so brave today."

My stomach twisted a little with unease. Had I been? I'd been running away, with Horace, because the prospect of witnessing Hank's wedding to another was too unbearable. Was that brave? There were things I didn't know how to explain to Hank.

Hank shook his head, and his eyes grew hard. "You brought justice to that coward Ario. What a lowlife. He risked the lives of his people and...." Hank huffed. "Well, he'll get what he deserves. And you made that happen." He smiled at me. I flashed him a weak grin, then looked away, pretending to be interested in the fireworks.

I swallowed against the lump in my throat. Only Iggy, of all my friends, knew the truth. Would the others accept it? Would Hank? I wanted to believe that he'd understand my need to meet my brother and get to know him. I hoped he'd understand that Horace as a person to me wasn't the same Horace who would unleash a monster on innocent people —that I hadn't known he would do such a thing. But would he throw me in the same boat as Ario? Would he think me a fool for trusting Horace? Was I one? I bit my lip, hard.

I'd had my reasons to trust him; Horace wasn't all bad. He'd saved me as a child, and we still hadn't solved the mystery we'd uncovered in Wee Ferngroveshire. Was Horace onto a political conspiracy to cover up the attack at Monsters Rise? That couldn't be completely discounted... at least in my eyes. I folded my arms and hugged myself. A firework exploded into the shapes of the sun and the moon.

Besides, if Horace hadn't disrupted the wedding, Hank would be married to Shaday right now. These fireworks would be in celebration of their marriage. He had been prepared to go through with it. If anything, in a weird way, we owed Horace for our chance to be together now. I glanced sideways up at Hank as he watched the lights in the sky. I doubted he'd see it that way.

My stomach twisted further. And now I had my brother to worry about. Would he be out for revenge on me for foiling his plans and exposing some of his secrets?

I glanced left and caught Hank's mother, brother, and sister-in-law all watching me. They turned hurriedly away, except for the sister-in-law—I thought her name was Emmaline. She flashed me a big grin and waved her fingers at me. Hank's father glared down at the celebrating, dancing, parading citizens below. And that was another thing. With our relationship public, I'd probably be seeing a lot more of Hank's family and need to polish up on my royal etiquette—of which I knew none. I sighed, my emotions churning inside me.

On one hand I wanted to cheer along with the rest of them. Shaday would rule and bring more equality and strength to the throne of the Fire Kingdom, and now Hank and I had a chance of being together. On the other, I had a murderous brother who may or may not want to punish me. As well, I had a boyfriend who'd nearly chosen to be with another out of obligation to his dysfunctional family (not that I could judge) and lots of secrets weighing me down.

I thought back to what I'd said to Hank a few moments ago. I *was* more hopeful now... wasn't I?

DID YOU ENJOY FULL MOONS, DUNES & MACAROONS?

You can make a huge difference!

1. **Leave a review on Amazon.** It's the best way to help indie authors, like me, by helping other readers discover the book.

2. Go to www.ErinJohnsonWrites.com and **sign up to my mailing list.** You'll always know when the next book's coming out, and I'll let you know about fun giveaways and special deals. **Plus, I'll send you** *Imogen's Spellbook*, **a custom illustrated collection of recipes featured in the story.**

3. Check out book 6, available summer 2018!

STAY UP-TO-DATE BY SIGNING UP FOR THE ERIN JOHNSON WRITES NEWSLETTER

Sign up for the Erin Johnson Writes newsletter
at
www.ErinJohnsonWrites.com

As a thank you for signing up, you'll receive
Imogen's Spellbook
a free book of illustrated recipes featured in
The Spells & Caramels Series.

A NOTE FROM THE AUTHOR

I've always dreamed of being a published author, and to realize that dream, and have people like you actually read my book—I can't tell you how much it means to me. So, truly, thank you.

If you enjoyed the story, and you'd like to help me as an author, please leave me a review on Amazon. It doesn't matter how long or short, a review is the very best way you can help me stay in business and keep writing. Plus, you'll help other readers discover Imogen and her adventures.

Thanks so much,
Erin

ABOUT THE AUTHOR

A native of Tempe, Arizona, Erin spends her time crafting mysterious, magical, romance-filled stories that'll hopefully make you laugh. This is her fifth book.

In between, she's traveling, napping with her dogs, eating with her friends and family, and teaching Pilates (to allow her to eat more).

Erin loves to hear from readers! You can contact her here:
erin@erinjohnsonwrites.com

facebook.com/EJohnsonWrites
twitter.com/EJohnsonWrites

Printed in Great Britain
by Amazon